A Year of Spanish

by

Cora Grove Clarke

This is a work of fiction. Names, characters, places, and incidents are products of the author's imagination or are used fictitiously and are not to be construed as real. Any resemblance to actual events, locales, organizations, or persons, living or dead, is entirely coincidental.

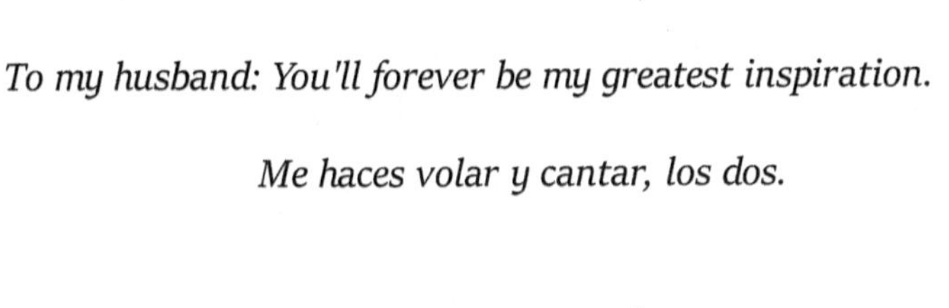
To my husband: You'll forever be my greatest inspiration.

Me haces volar y cantar, los dos.

uno

"CAN WE GO TO THE bookstore later? I want to pick up another novel to practice translating with."

Hayley pulled a face at me, raking her blonde hair out of her eyes. "Seriously, Alyssa, we only have two weeks left of summer and you wanna waste it studying?" She was sitting cross-legged on my bed, picking through a pile of my clean clothes to swipe and add to her own personal collection. "Next summer is gonna be, y'know, getting ready for college and all that. We should just chill and enjoy our last remnants of free time. Besides," she added, looking up from one of my old hoodies, "there is an end-of-summer barbecue being put on by the Baptist church tomorrow night. If you wanna put up with the sermon in the middle, there's going to be a pool and free food. Plus, I heard Shawn is going to be there with a couple of his friends, so..." She waggled her eyebrows at me.

I scoffed and continued pulling clothes out of my closet. "Senior year is the final lap before the finish line, and I'm not about to compromise my nearly perfect GPA chasing frivolous things like relationships."

"Lame."

I rolled my eyes. "Or caring what other people think of me."

"You sound like your Mom when you talk like that," Hayley replied flippantly. "I mean, you've put in your time. Your GPA will be *fine* if you just let yourself relax for once. Come on, it's our senior year! One last chance to finally enjoy ourselves. Find some romance, eh?" She threw one shoulder forward and shimmied it in an attempt to appear sexy.

I laughed at her attempt to lighten the mood, but I didn't answer her. I caught my reflection in the mirror above my dresser. Sunken-in hazel eyes half-hidden behind a curtain of straight, brown hair. The color was too ashy. My nose was too big. Was I pretty? I didn't know. Nobody had ever bothered to clarify that for me. Oh, how I wanted...

"Ugh, what is *this?*"

I snapped out of my self-pity to see Hayley holding

up a black dress with a matronly white collar. "Oh, that's one of the dresses Mom made me wear during her city council campaign functions last year."

"Yikes. I'm sorry they had to see you like that, *Fraülein Maria*."

"Yeah, well, got to keep up appearances. After all, I'm the 'face of the virtuous youth of Lynn Creek.'"

Snort. "*Pfft*. Virtuous." She balled up the dress and chucked it across the room, aiming for my paper bin and missing by three feet, knocking Dapper out of his napping spot in the window sill.

"Aw, baby! She didn't mean to," I cooed at the flying black ball of fur as he fled through the door to escape. I scooped up the dress and turned back to Hayley. "Thanks for scarring my cat for life."

She shrugged.

Having returned the dress to the darkest corner of my closet, I fished out my windbreaker. "Are you done going through my stuff so can we go the bookstore, then?"

She sighed loudly and pretended to melt off the bed. She continued her protest on the floor, body flopped in melodrama. "Why do I have to take you? Just ask your dad to borrow the car this weekend."

"Because," I answered, searching for my purse. "I

want to get as much Spanish practice in before Spanish III this semester. Señora Barkett warned me that she wasn't sure which of the three candidates the school board chose to be her replacement, so I'm playing it safe."

"And she told you this when?"

"We met up for coffee last month."

"You're certifiable, you know that? Spending your precious summer time hanging out with a teacher."

"Hardly. Last year was her first year teaching."

"My point still stands."

I opened my mouth to protest but thought the better of it. I wanted to defend Barkett. Besides Hayley, she was one of the few people in high school that I would have considered a friend. She was fresh out of college and shared the same love of show-tunes and music that I did. So during that summer we had already met up a handful of times to chat and exchange favorite albums. *Why* did she have to go get married and have a baby?

Hayley picked herself off the floor with a groan. "I dunno, this just seems like overkill. Aren't you already like an 'A' student? You'll be fine."

"Well, maybe I just like Spanish."

"Really? I couldn't wait to get out of French. What's

so special about Spanish?"

"It just makes sense to me. The rules never change. Once I learn the basics of pronunciation, I can literally pick up something I've never read before and say it perfectly. There's something kind of comforting about that."

That seemed to make sense to Hayley, and she shrugged in agreement. "Okay, point taken. Still, you're talking about a trip all the way into Dukwibal Bay. What do I get out of this?"

"I'll buy you a book, too. Your choice."

"Hmm." It was an irresistible bribe, and finally she grabbed her backpack and keys off my bed. "Fine. I'll get myself some design books. I've been wanting to re-do my room, and my Mom gave the go ahead to do whatever I want."

"Perfect. I'll feed your whim if you feed mine."

* * *

BOOKSTORE CHAINS WERE STARTING TO disappear across the country, but we were pretty lucky that modernity had yet to touch our corner of the Pacific Northwest. Our local Brooks & Campbell branch was alive and well, surprisingly busy for a Thursday evening. Being a card-holding member, I easily located a copy of *500 Spanish Verbs,* briefly stopping and checking to make sure

Hayley was happily installed in the Art and Design section.

The Spanish Fiction section was smaller than I would have liked, but I was still happy that we had any at all, especially since the Spanish speaking population was still only a growing minority in my agriculture-heavy county.

I had already picked through the juvenile literature, and was feeling in the mood for something more toothsome. I picked up a copy of *Amor en el Tiempo de Colera*, reading the synopsis on the back of cover. One of the words I didn't quite recognize, and I was leafing through the *Verb* book when suddenly a soft question from nearby broke my concentration.

"Do you like Gabriel Garcia Marquez?"

In the fluorescent lighting I could tell that he had an olive complexion, one that you would associate with someone well acquainted with the sun. Experience had already marked his face, telling me that he was not my age, but nothing in his gait insisted to me that he was old by any means. As he got closer, I had to look up considerably to take in the rest of him. Strong jaw, cropped chocolate hair, dark brown eyes...

Those eyes, they were more black than brown, the kind that sucked you in.

I can't imagine what my face was doing in that

moment, but I was shocked enough by the fact that a guy, a handsome one at that, had somehow addressed me directly. On purpose. Looking behind me briefly, there was no one else in our aisle. He was definitely talking to me. By this time, I had already forgotten what he had even asked me. I gaped at him stupidly.

He shuffled his books into the crook of one of his arms and indicated with a free hand what I was holding, "Have you read Marquez before?"

I looked down at the thick volume. Breaking eye contact somehow made my brain start cycling again. "Yeah, I've read a couple. I really liked *One Hundred Years of Solitude*, but that was in English. I thought I'd read this one next. See what he's like in his original Spanish."

He must have noticed my *Verb* book, because the following "hmm" was one of indecision. "Marquez is great, but I would really warn you that unless you're already fluent, it's going to be very stop-and-go if you still have to use a reference."

Stubbornness flared up in me, and handsome or not, I wasn't going to let anyone tell me what I wasn't capable of. I hugged the volume closer to myself, tilting my head up with what little pride I had. "I think I'll manage just fine. Thank you."

"You sure? Because if you're interested in the whole star-crossed subject and want something a little bit smoother..." He was already scanning the shelves, pulling out another book. "I would think you would probably like Laura Esquive-"

"I'm good." I interrupted, a bit breathless. His search had brought him closer to my eye level, and the proximity was making me dazed.

He tilted his head to look back at me, one corner of his lip turning up. His expression was one of both amusement and exasperation. "Are you...?"

I never got to hear the rest of his question.

"There you are! You ready to go?" Hayley barreled around the corner, completely ignorant of my conversation, throwing a couple coffee-table sized books in my direction. "I can't decide between these two books so I guess you're buying both for me."

In the shuffle of trying to catch her books and reorient myself, the stranger had already stepped a couple feet back and returned to his original task. I threw a glance back at him as Hayley started dragging me toward the checkout. His head was down again, and I was disappointed that I couldn't at least have the pleasure of his eye contact one last time.

I shook it off as we checked out, and Hayley carried me away to the car with a one-sided conversation about barbecues, Shawn, and the last summer of our high school lives.

dos

FALL IS ALREADY REARING ITS head in Washington State by the time August comes to a close. I watched as fellow students paraded around in their finest, an odd mixture of sweaters and tank tops on this first day of school, everyone confused on how to dress in this seasonal convergence. I knew the coolness of the morning was a ruse; already layers were peeling off as the chill and fog burned off in the heat of the summer afternoon. I sat on the side benches of the administrative hallway, a spectator, Hayley bouncing eagerly next to me. Her focus was scattered, first pointing out one person's clothing choice, then moving on to comment on who was dating who.

"Ooh, Alyssa, look!" She pointed at a nearby couple. "Check out Kat and Graham! Didn't they break up last year?" She asked me while quickly tucking her blonde hair behind her ear, smiling shyly as her crush du-jour passed by.

To be honest, I couldn't answer her. What anyone else was up to never seemed to be any of my business. But I looked at the couple at the end of the hallway; they were holding hands. Kat was laughing at some passing remark of Graham's, their heads tilted together in unison. The rest of the world was locked out and uninvited to their private joke. I sat there wishing. Wishing that for myself...

Focus, Alyssa, came my mother's voice. *Don't get caught up in the present...*

I thought back to the night before. My parents had held a pep rally of sorts, forcing me to listen to the same speech that I heard at the beginning of every school year. Mom was sitting at the dining room table, dad pacing behind her like an agitated football coach.

"Focus, Alyssa," My mom said, one finger pointing at me. "Don't get caught up in the present..."

"...Continually prepare for the future. I know, I know..." I rolled my eyes, elbows on the table, chin pressing into my hands.

Dad stopped moving, his gray beard twitching. He could see my boredom, and maybe he was starting to feel bad for me. "I know that you've heard all of this before,

'Lys, but this is the home stretch. There's a great temptation to sink into 'senioritis.'" This was accompanied by air quotations, and I couldn't help but smirk.

Mom cut back in, brushing some hair back from her messy bun. "The main thing is that you stay the course. SAT prep, college applications, your cumulative grade point average. All of these things affect the *rest of your life*, and with your track record, you have absolutely *no* excuse for lagging behind now."

"With my track record, you would think you would trust me by now," I commented dryly.

Mom wasn't happy with my apparent lack of concern last night, but my parents both knew that their speech once again hit its target. I had squared my resolve.

The bell rang, indicating that our final period was about to start. I stood up, only to find myself ducking quickly to avoid a hasty freshman with a backpack swinging wildly. Hayley groaned and pulled her bag over her shoulder, looking at her course schedule. "Math, yuck. At the end of the day, too..." she glanced quickly over her shoulder, some student at the end of the hall catching her eye. I looked behind me as well, but as Hayley was a head taller than me, my view was only a wall of bodies. "Of course," she said sarcastically, "Bethany *would* have the most ridiculous leather boots, wouldn't she? All that money and she *still* looks like a tacky bitch." Her tone was derisive, but I could hear the barely-concealed longing in her voice. Hayley had an insatiable desire to be seen, a desire that I didn't share or understand, and I found myself wondering when she was going to stop wishing she was someone else. It was becoming increasingly difficult to spend any time with her without feeling exhausted by her constant commentary on the *salacious* lives of the upper crust of Lynn Creek High School. Still, I had to remind myself, loyal friends were hard to come by when you were straight-laced like me. The path I walked didn't always put me in the good graces of my peers, and Hayley was all I had.

Hayley's math class was toward the rear of the campus and my path immediately diverged from hers. I quickly said goodbye in her direction and parted ways, heading out into the courtyard that would take me to the language wing. There was a notable lack of actual hallways in this school; only two of them were indoors. The rest of the classrooms were only accessible via outdoor courtyards. The idiot who designed this building clearly lived somewhere desert-like; no Washingtonian would subject students to the elements between every class period. As it was today, however, the sun hit my eyes, making it hard to read my crumpled schedule. Under "Kessler, Alyssa" was a list of the four classes I would take during this semester's block schedule.

<u>Period One: Economics</u> – Mr. Turpin

Mr. Turpin's voice was monotone and droning. A terrible way to start the morning.

<u>Period Two: English</u> – Mrs. Draper

Our first reading assignment was Othello. Shakespeare was a cinch. So far, so good.

<u>Period Three: U.S. History</u> – Ms. Rabenstein

Hayley shared this class with me. It was hard to get her to shut up the entire time.

<u>Period Four: Spanish Level 3</u> – Mr. Brown

I frowned at the teacher's name and heaved a sigh of frustration before entering the classroom.

Sure enough, the entire room had been redecorated, all traces of Señora Barkett gone. Even her Spanish labels for things were missing, the ones she had written in little bubble letters. Now there was nothing above the flag cheerfully reminding me that it was a *bandera,* and I felt a keen sense of loss.

In the place of Señora's happy posters, the traditional maps of the Latin world were hung up at even intervals, two in front flagging the white board. The rest of the room was devoid of any other personal touches. It felt sterile. I at once felt suspicious of this Mr. Brown character.

An image was painting itself in my mind of a short, squat man with coke-bottle glasses, devoid of any fun or personality. Was I doomed to sub-par teaching and busy work the entire year? Sighing, I prepared myself to be miserable.

Since I was the first one to arrive and the room was empty, I dug into my backpack, looking over the assignment I was given for my history class. Soon other students started filing in, some looking just as worried as I was about the already piling homework load. All of the faces were recognizable, and I recited their Spanish nicknames as they came in.

Paco. Real name Isaac. Avid wrestler.

Katalina, otherwise known as Kristin Webber and my polar opposite in every way. It was surprising to me that she was continuing into the higher Spanish levels. There wasn't an indication that she had an interest in the subject, as far as I was aware.

Sancho. The one and only. I couldn't even remember his real name, seeing as he was a junior and I had only ever attended Spanish II with him last year.

Pedro and Yolanda came in together. No big surprise. Yolanda always managed to attach herself to the latest and greatest, and Pedro was a varsity linebacker this year.

Armando, Consuelo, Mateo y Ramon... Besides myself, nine other students were in attendance. Higher-level Spanish classes were always smaller than the ones below, since most students only took their two required years of foreign language and then proceeded to forget everything they learned. There was a small comfort in knowing that my fellow students in this class were (mostly) serious about continuing their Spanish education.

I chose a seat at the front of the class, fishing out a pencil and an empty notebook, ready for whatever this teacher was going to throw at me. With a new teacher came the task of learning how to impress him. Catering to a teacher's likes and dislikes were part of the arsenal of a good student, after all. The door behind us opened and closed, and I turned to get a first look at my target.

I blinked.

Whatever expectations I had were completely obliterated. The man who approached the front of the classroom was nothing like the bumbling figure that I had imagined. Looking down at my schedule again, I read his name again. Mr. Brown.

Tall.

Handsome.

Familiar.

He made his way to the podium, walking with

purpose, weight directed into the floor with each step as if he had walked down these aisles with a familiarity that I know he did not possess.

I dared a brief glance up at him as he passed. His pace slowed almost imperceptibly, and his eyes met mine. I saw that instant spark of recognition flare up within his gaze before it was expertly tamped down. Confused by this turn of events, I felt strange under his gaze. As he continued forward, I quietly shifted in my seat, folding my arms in front of me. I shook my head to mentally reset, trying to prepare for whatever lay ahead.

The second bell rang, announcing the beginning of class, and Mr. Brown followed cue.

"Bueno, ¡bienvenidos al tercer curso de español!" (Welcome to third-level Spanish!) He greeted us warmly, sweeping his eyes across the entire group, treating us all to a grin. It was lop-sided, I noted, and extremely adorable. He was visibly excited on this first day of classes, and his energy seemed to burn brighter than the students he was currently addressing. "I am Señor Brown, and as you probably guessed, I am new to Lynn Creek High School. I only just moved here from California, so I beg your future indulgence if I complain about the ludicrous amount of rain here." He turned, deliberated before settling on a blue marker, and wrote his name on the white board in a slanted penmanship, followed by bullet points.

Señor Brown

- *Nuevo (New)*

- *No le gusta la lluvia (Does not like rain)*

He paused, thought about it for a moment, and added one more point.

- *Super-impresionante (Super-awesome)*

He turned back to us. "I don't know where each of you are skill-wise, and I'll be figuring that out in the days to come, but be prepared for a different kind of class compared to the basic levels you've already taken. We're going to spend a good amount of time discussing the people, the history, the customs... Things are different in the Latin world," He leaned on the podium in a nonchalant manner. "You're never going to understand the language, and just how beautiful it is, unless you learn these things first." The wistfulness in his voice was accompanied by a look that willed us to fully understand his meaning.

He continued, and the longer he continued to speak, the more it became apparent to me that this wasn't a man that just taught Spanish as a job. He ate, slept, and *breathed* the culture. It wasn't enough to him that we understood the basic grammar and memorized the vocabulary lists. As he explained this to us he glowed, and it was obvious that he had a passion for what he was teaching. It was infectious. I forgot my previous awkwardness and found myself sitting upright, ready to hear more.

He had already moved on to learning each of our names, starting with those who, despite the small number of students, chose to sit in the very back. What is your name? And what is your Spanish nickname? I wasn't paying attention and I missed Sancho's real name again.

He checked them off one by one on the attendance sheet. Finally, he reached the front row, and I was the last one to be introduced.

"Y tú. ¿Como te llamas?" He looked down at me, pencil poised in his hand.

With his attention squarely on me, I felt that same disorientation. For a second I forgot who I was, but I recovered quickly. "Me llamo Alyssa Kessler, pero mi nombre español es Julietta." (My name is Alyssa Kessler, but my Spanish name is Julietta.)

He checked me off his list, looking back up at me with a smile. "Es un placer a conocerte, Julietta." (Pleasure to meet you, Julietta.)

Again, my brain supplied.

A blush flashed through my cheeks, and I knew right then and there that it was settled. I was determined to be the best damn student he had ever laid eyes on.

tres

THE FIRST COUPLE WEEKS WERE a blur of teachers trying to pick up the pieces after a summer that destroyed all retention of what was taught the previous year. Mrs. Draper had discovered the collective loss of any knowledge of the seven uses of commas. This had resulted in proof-reading assignments that were as mind-numbing as they were necessary. U.S History was currently focused on the events leading to the Revolutionary War, and an essay with references was already due in the near future.

There wasn't any respite from the onslaught of assignments, and I tried my best to keep up with them. It took the majority of my evenings, even without Hayley calling in complete panic about her math homework. Explanations over the phone were sometimes not enough, and occasionally I had to set everything to the side and dodge out of the house and run up the street to flip through Hayley's textbook with her. I hated logarithms in junior year, and I appreciated them even less the second time around. Somehow everything got done, but it left me very little free time. If it could be called that.

My remaining energy was expended on fending off my mother. She had mysteriously found some free time away from her seat on Lynn Creek city council to research which academic clubs looked best on college applications. She spent every weekend in September trying to convince me to run for student body president, which I persistently shot down. My mother clearly didn't understand where I stood on the social ladder.

The easiest part of my week was Spanish class. We were covering old ground, reviewing tenses of verb forms and random vocabulary lists. Señor Brown was clearly testing the waters in order to determine where he needed to pick up the reins and start introducing new concepts. All of this came naturally enough to me, my continued Spanish exercises throughout the summer paying off. I hadn't lost as much as some of the students who clearly had an active social life. While Pedro and Yolanda were struggling to remember the difference between the preterite and imperfect forms of past-tense, I was freed up to satisfy my curiosity about my new teacher.

I was too scared to ask about our first meeting, and

beyond the first day, nothing in his manner suggested that he would acknowledge it. Thankfully, other questions seemed okay to ask, and mine were only a few in the barrage that he received from all of us Spanish III students; any new teacher was familiar with this treatment.

Where in California are you from?

San Consuelo, Southern California.

Are you married?

No.

Can you teach us how to insult someone's mother in Spanish? (That question came from Sancho)

Yes, but I won't.

It seemed any question that was put to him was answered, as long as it was asked in Spanish. It became a hobby of mine to find out as much about him as possible, and even after the rest of the class lost interest, I continued to ask questions. In the last couple sessions, I had already established that he spoke four languages (English, Spanish, French, and Italian), that he had studied in Costa Rica and Spain, and that he was into a variety of outdoor sports, especially biking and kayaking. It was apparent, too. Finely defined muscles were discernible underneath the cotton button-up that he frequently wore, a fact that I found hard to ignore sitting in the front row. The more questions I asked, it seemed, the more he fascinated me, so I knew that as long as he kept answering my questions, I would keep asking them.

On this particular afternoon, I was determined to finish the exam well ahead of anyone else to free up some question time. The rest of the class was still busy struggling to complete it, heads bent over their work. I checked over my answers one more time before heading to Señor's desk at the back of the room.

A couple weeks' time had brought about some additions to the classroom, some personal touches that showed Mr. Brown was just as adverse to the barren classroom setting as I was. Two days in, a CD player appeared on the front counter, along with a haphazard pile of discs. Study time was now accompanied by music from every corner of the Latin world, ranging from Dominican merengue to Argentinian techno. Today's addition was a picture series of his travels in frames set carefully across the table under the back window. I took a moment to appreciate one photo where the camera was apparently set on the ground with a self-timer, Señor's figure tiny and blurred, dwarfed next to the towering statue of Christ the Redeemer.

With the rest of the students occupied, he was presently at his desk, taking the opportunity to plan a lesson for a level one class. He was wearing reading glasses that only seemed to appear on his nose when he was working with paperwork. His head sprang up though when my exam fluttered down on the desk and into his view. "¿Ya estás terminada?" (Finished already?)

I nodded, folding my hands behind my back. "¿Puedo hacer otra pregunta?" (Can I ask you another question?)

By now he had begun to expect my daily questions, so he put his papers aside and folded his hands neatly on top of his desk, looking amused. "¿Cómo no? Preguntala." (Why not? Ask away.)

I had given this one some thought, so I plowed on ahead. "¿Cuándo decidiste que querías enseñar a español?" (When did you decide that you wanted to teach Spanish?)

He waggled his head back and forth as if he was giving some serious thought to the question. "Creo que tenía catorce años. He vistado México con un grupo de joventud de mi iglesia. Me di cuenta de que hay una necesidad de la gente a aprender español de modo que pueden ayudar más eficazmente." (I believe I was fourteen. I visited Mexico with my church's youth group. I realized that there was a need for people to learn Spanish so that they could help more effectively.)

I was impressed. "Una causa noble." (A noble cause.) It was not every day that you met someone that managed to follow through with such a conviction.

My thoughts must been obvious on my face, because

he rewarded me with a smirk. "Soy yo. *Tan* noble," (That's me. *So* noble.) He teased.

The only noise for some moments was the ticking clock and the skittering of pencil lead across multiple desks. He looked back down at his desk, glasses sliding down his bridge slightly. "So," he asked quietly, breaking his own rule of Spanish-only during session. "How's that Marquez working out for you?"

I huffed in surprise that he finally broke that barrier, but I could see his quirked eyebrow. I was being teased again. "It's going," I replied with impudence. In reality, only two total pages were translated before I furiously gave up, but there was no way to admit that he was right without giving him satisfaction.

My answer rang false to him. "You should have taken my advice, you know," he chided, a perfect picture of the cat who got the cream.

Curiosity settled deep in my stomach. There was a response sitting on the tip of my tongue, but by that time other students were getting up to turn in their exams, so I excused myself and went back to my desk, turning some things over in my head. We still had ten minutes to go until the end of class, but since Mr. Brown had no more lessons for the day, I busied myself with packing my bags and planning my next series of questions that I would attack him with tomorrow.

When the final bell rung, I was all set to leave, since Hayley was waiting to give me a ride home so we could have a study group. Something stopped me, though. A question suddenly occurred to me, one that simply couldn't wait until tomorrow.

So instead of running out the door with the other students, I stayed behind.

Mr. Brown was still sitting at his desk, lost in his work, his dark eyes flitting across the information on each page. I lingered near the back of the room near the door, taking the chance to drink him in, just appreciating the ability to watch him without his knowing it. But after a moment, he must have felt my presence, because he looked up at me, an expression of pure curiosity on his face. "Yes, Julietta?"

I was suddenly aware that I was in the room alone with him. For a moment, I questioned my motives, whether or not this question was a good idea. My muscles tightened, the first sign of panic seizing my frame. I reminded myself to take a breath. "Tengo uno más pregunta." (I have one more question.)

He pulled a face at me. "¿Otra? ¿Qué es esto, un interrogatorio?" (Another? What is this, an interrogation?) He let out a laugh, his annoyance clearly not genuine.

"*Sí*, otra." His humor had eased my anxiety, and I

felt brave in that moment. I made my move before my courage failed me. "¿Cuantos años tienes?" (How old are you?)

He stopped putting his papers away in a manila folder. "¿En serio?" (Seriously?)

I nodded. "En serio."

He waved the question off and laughed. "*Viejo*, Julietta." (*Old*, Julietta.)

I rolled my eyes at him. "Humor me, Señor," I said, forgetting my Spanish.

He considered me for a second before answering. "Trienta y tres." (33)

I thought about that for a second, trying to decide if that was a problem or not. My response came quickly once I noticed that he seemed to be measuring my reaction. "No eres viejo." (You aren't old.)

It was his turn to forget his Spanish. "Oh, really?" His teasing tone returned. "And how old are you, oh wise Julietta?" He grinned lopsidedly, clearly enjoying poking fun at me.

I felt that the counter-question was slightly unfair, but I answered anyway. "Eighteen." I shifted on the balls of my feet.

"Aha." He answered, as if that explained everything. "See, Julietta? I'm *viejo*."

I must have appeared frustrated, because he stood up and walked over to where I was standing, looking very much like he wanted to change the subject. He took his reading glasses off and held them in his hand, taking a seat on one of the desks that was near me. It seemed uneven with me continuing to stand while he was sitting so close, so I also situated myself on top of a desk, noticing every inch of our height difference as my feet swung off the edge.

Mr. Brown twirled his glasses absentmindedly by one of the temples. "Listen..."

Oh here it goes, I thought. My skin was already flushing from the future embarrassment.

But then I was wrong.

"I don't know what you're planning to study in the future, and it's only been a couple weeks into this semester, but," He folded his arms, leaning forward towards me. "I am planning an advanced placement course in the spring, and you have a lot of potential, Julietta. It would be a pleasure to have you in that class, if you'd consider it."

I reddened further, not used to receiving many compliments at all, and certainly not ones from handsome strangers-turned-teachers. "Thank you." Hiding my nervous energy by tucking my hair behind my ears, I added, "You know, I'm planning on minoring in Spanish when I get into college." I didn't mention that I had come to this decision only recently, for reasons I wasn't ready to admit to myself.

"Good for you," He said and quietly looked at me for a minute. His gaze was doing weird things to me again. I wanted to look back at him, but those eyes of his were so piercing that I felt if I made contact for too long, he would either find his way into my thoughts, or just simply melt me, one or the other. So I looked down at the carpet, watching my feet swing in and out of my view.

Another moment passed, and when I couldn't stand it any longer, I hoisted myself off the desk and picked up my backpack. My feet slowly carried me backwards towards the door. "Pues, hasta mañana, Señor!" I waved a weak goodbye in his direction, not watching where I was going. When I started to trip, I turned to see the edge of the mat that my foot was caught on. I ducked and corrected myself, turning around and laying my hand on the door handle, embarrassed and ready to flee the scene.

He chuckled and stood up, finding his way down the row of desks and heading back to his own, picking up the pile of half-corrected papers. He slipped the glasses back on, and all I could think of was how intelligent and *sexy* he looked in that moment. He smiled, and I stared. "Adios,

Julietta," he called to me.

I smiled at him and fumbled with the door. My racing thoughts made it difficult to focus on such a simple task, but finally I was able to grasp the handle and yank the door open. My mouth was fixed in a grin of sheer embarrassment. "Adios, Señor." I replied, mad at myself for acting like an idiot. I quickly stepped out and made my way down the courtyard, a bit jarred.

Two things were now clear to me: My fascination was quickly getting out of hand. Also, I don't know if I imagined it, but I could have sworn that his eyes were on my back as I left the room.

Imaginations, if left to run wild, have a habit of becoming very dangerous.

cuatro

LYNN CREEK'S HARVEST FESTIVAL BLUSTERED into town as suddenly as the fallen leaves. The buildings downtown were revitalized with strings of orange and yellow flags, and scarecrows flagged the sides of every business entrance. Our town was always a layover for tourists on the way to more glamorous destinations like Seattle, but October was an especially busy month for us. The streets, which were normally designed for the everyday traffic of only 7,000 people, were now crowded with poorly parked cars and jaywalkers attempting to make their way to the hay maze and food tents.

When I was little, I liked the caramel apples and pumpkin patches as much as the next kid. As a teenager though, I had learned that this time of the year was a quiet reprieve from my parents. Mom was working in tandem with the city Chamber of Commerce to handle the mass of people, and every year my dad was inevitably lured away from his custom home plans to help with set-up and tear-down. In the meantime, I was free to spread out into the living room, happily working on homework assignments with Latin pop blasting through the home surround sound.

As autumn ran its course, school life had been reduced to its normal tedium, with the exception of Spanish III. Through my regular "interrogations" (as Mr. Brown continued to call them) and through his avid lessons, Mr. Brown was revealing himself to be a source of endless fascination to me, and my interest in his life was nothing short of obsession. As a side-effect, the more time I spent in his class, the more my desire to achieve grew. It simply wasn't enough anymore to get the grade; I wanted to be the best, to hold that place of honor in his esteem. Mr. Brown needed to *see* me. Settling for being just another student was, well, wholly unacceptable.

I couldn't help but laugh when he talked about his own experiences going through high school Spanish, how one of his teachers taught the class cheesy pick-up lines and always wore orange polyester slacks everyday (Did he have multiple pairs, or did he wash the one every night? Or did he wash them at all? It was a mystery.) He ticked off a list of his favorite bands and revealed himself to be a fan of punk-rock, new-wave, and (here he blushed) big-hair metal.

He talked about his world travels, how in Spain he had his first taste of authentic paella and his first exposure to flamenco dancing. It conjured up images in my head of swirling skirts and the heady scents of a Mediterranean night. You could see vivacity of life radiating off of him as he answered question after question, and I was enthralled.

My enthusiastic dedication to him manifested itself in a variety of desperate attempts to please him and associate myself with the subject he held so dear. I delved headlong into the intricacies of the Latin world. In addition to the regular assignments, I found myself taking extra time to study Spanish and Latin American history and art. I couldn't wait to see the look of delight on Mr. Brown's face when I arrived in class with some new tidbit that I had researched. He was intrigued that I was taking such an extracurricular interest in his subject, praising me in front of everyone for my initiative.

"Muy bien, Julietta"

It was a craved compliment, and I was never tired of hearing it. I would blush and thank him as if it was nothing.

It was really *everything.*

The sheer amount of praise I was receiving wasn't beyond my classmates' notice either, and it wasn't beyond *my* notice the jealous looks that were being aimed in my direction. Whispers of "teacher's pet" were being thrown around behind my back, uttered in a false whisper meant to travel. That particular title was one that I had been carrying for years, but for the first time, it didn't seem to phase me. My classmates didn't understand. How could they possibly know? It was Mr. Brown's approval, not grades or pride, that was my ultimate drive. My energy source was fueled by his very presence. He became my reason for the class, the highlight of my every day. If I ever disappointed him in any way, the end result would surely be devastation.

But just as I was making my way to the top of the class, to the point where I thought that I was truly untouchable, I had to go and do something stupid.

What goes up must inevitably come down, as they say.

I always had the habit of saying things before thinking. It was not uncommon for my bluntness to offend those around me. Once I messed up, however, every consecutive sentence tumbling out of my mouth only managed to dig me deeper. It was one of my quirks that I had never been very happy with.

It was nearing the end of the class period on a cool

fall Friday. As Mr. Brown was finishing writing out some notes on the overhead for the next class, quiet study had slowly devolved into idle chatter, no one really paying attention to the paperwork they were given.

Paco and Sancho were having a heated discussion on one side of the room, debating on the pros and cons of using whey powder as a bulking technique in their muscle-building regimen. Yolanda was on the sidelines throwing adoring looks in the direction of Sancho, who was rolling up his sleeves to prove his point. I rolled my eyes as I finished my homework. Tucking the finished sheets into a notebook in my backpack, I sat back and enjoyed a moment to myself.

My wandering eyes started to settle in one particular direction, and, not wanting to be caught too long contemplating the shadows that the overhead light was casting across Mr. Brown's nose and jaw, I turned about in my chair, thinking I had better make an attempt to make small talk with the students behind me. It was a small feat to work my way into the conversation initially; over the last few years an erroneous conclusion was made that my lack of social interaction was due to contempt on my part, which caused many to ostracize me. Oddly enough, Pedro and Katalina were feeling charitable that day.

Katalina, the blonde cornerstone of the gossip circuit in Lynn Creek High School, never took too kindly to me.

Somehow, though, I had never been one of the subjects of her nasty rumors, which I suspected had something to do with the fact that I had frequently helped her both in Spanish and Economics class. Pedro, with his disproportionately large shoulders and devil-may-care attitude, seemed to be the quintessential jock, playing in both the football and basketball seasons. Yet despite his appearance, he was deceptively smart, and quite often gave me a run for my money in English class. There was an unspoken amount of respect between us, so when I joined the discussion, the friendliness wasn't entirely a show of politeness.

October was in its final week, yet summer was still fresh on the brains of many students, and the conversation started revolving around what we had done during our summer vacation. Eventually this led to us sharing our memories of last year's Spanish class, having a laugh over the insufferable but catchy Spanish songs that Señora Barkett had taught us in our first couple years together.

The last time I had coffee with her, Señora Barkett had brought her new baby boy with her, wrapped around her middle in a muslin cocoon. I told the group about this, telling them how she was and how beautiful her new baby was. Somehow, without my brain's permission, my mouth began to launch into the story of Señora's worries about the education board's selection process. Perhaps it was the fact that I had the attention of my peers, a rare occurrence, but the story continued to spill out.

"She said that she didn't like the finalists they chose to replace her with," I informed the group. Almost immediately after I had mentioned this, however, I covered my mouth with my hand, mentally chiding myself. I shouldn't have been talking about it. This was a private conversation I had with Mrs. Barkett, not for the other students to know. I too frequently spoke about things before even giving thought to who would hear it, and who would take it wrong.

I regretted I had ever said it.

"What are you guys talking about?" said a familiar voice behind me.

I spun around. There he was, not too far away. He had obviously heard our conversation, and had abandoned his work to quietly listen in. I made eye contact with him, and panic seized me. But it didn't seem to seize my tongue, taking the proverbial foot and shoving it further down my throat. "Our old teacher told me that you weren't her first choice as her replacement." I felt the words leave my mouth of their own volition, shocked by the cool tone with which they were delivered.

The look of disbelief and hurt that rippled across Mr. Brown's face and through his ebony eyes made me feel sick to my stomach. I looked down quickly, immediately ashamed. The quickest to react was Katalina, who was sitting behind me. She seized the opportunity to turn around and rebuked me. "Julietta, how mean of you! Mr. Brown is an awesome teacher!" She sneered and flipped her hair in an amplified motion, obviously enjoying herself. Other students had been looking for a way to make me look bad for weeks, and she had managed to claim the prize first.

Of course what she said was true. I wanted to tell him that I took it back and that he was the greatest teacher I had ever met. And the most wonderful man. That was clearly not an option. I didn't know what else to do, though, so I turned Katalina's comment to my advantage. I looked up at him again, trying to show complete repentance on my face. "Exactly! That was *her* opinion. I never said it was mine! You are *obviously* a great teacher, Mr. Brown." I threw my hands up in the air for emphasis, beside myself with worry. There was no way any compliment would erase what I had said, yet I held on to hope that he understood.

But it didn't work.

"Thank you," He replied distractedly, something akin to embarrassment flashing across his features. He tried to cover by an attempt at a neutral face, but I saw it there, the hurt, and I was utterly ruined by it. Mumbling an incoherent excuse, he ducked and went back to his work, but I knew that he wasn't paying attention to it. I could see his eyelids lowered, his dark orbs flitting back and forth, as if he was trying to figure something out in his head. I couldn't bear to look at him anymore and turned away.

The bell rung, cutting the tension. I had to get out of there. Grabbing my bag as quickly as possible, I rushed out of the door, pushing other students aside.

My mind was so overwhelmed with thoughts and regrets that how I got home was an incoherent blur. I must have taken the bus home, must have forced my fingers to enter the code that would let me in the house through the garage, because before I knew it, I was standing despondently in the middle of my room. I felt without direction, without a clue of what to do next. Surely not scream, which was what I wanted more than anything to do, but somehow couldn't. My hands hung at my sides, trembling for an outlet.

Dapper awoke from his nap and jumped down from my bed to wind between my legs, sensing my distress and attempting to comfort me. He caterwauled for me to pick him up, but I ignored him. The wheels of my mind were spinning out of control, searching for a way to process my misery. It was when his insistence turned into claws on my legs that I sunk down on the floor beside him, fingers twining into his fur. They twitched and resisted, but eventually my movements settled into a calming stroke. Appreciative purrs vibrated up my arm, and I closed my eyes and tried to sink myself into the sensation.

"I can't take this back. I can't fix this." I said to Dapper, to no one. Wrecked with helplessness, I buried my face in my hands. There was nothing I could possibly do could restore Mr. Brown's trust in me, I was certain.

But why did you care? My inner voice mocked. *After all, he's only a teacher. You're graduating and soon, it will all be over. He'll forget about it, and he'll forget about you. You're nothing special.* I took that truth and settled it deep in my chest.

As I tried sleeping that night, I continued telling myself that I was blowing everything out of proportion, but all I could see as I closed my eyes was his face, and the pain that marked his features disturbed me. I tossed until I gave up all hope of rest, lying awake through the night. I let the waves of despair wash over me, indulging in my self-pity.

What was wrong with me?

What had I done?

cinco

THE FOLLOWING MONDAY, I QUIETLY slipped in just as the bell rang, sliding between the rows, at once pulling out my homework as soon as I sat in my seat. I would have been unnoticeable except for the fact that it was not common for me to be silent in this class. That alone brought attention my way. I pretended to be absorbed in double-checking my work.

Mr. Brown entered the room and made a quick scan of the room, mentally taking attendance. My heartbeat rushed through my ears, panic tunneling my senses. I could see in my peripheral vision that he stopped on me a couple times before turning his attention to the first lessons of the period. I couldn't quite make out his expression.

The anxiety coursing through my veins made it nearly impossible to focus on what was going on around me. Taking control of my breathing required almost every ounce of my concentration. The textbook in front of me lost the definition of its edges as my sight blurred. It seemed that disassociation was proving to be a good coping mechanism, and the lesson and activity went on without my contribution for a good half hour before it finally registered that my name was being called.

"Julietta, ¿tienes la respuesta?"

I looked up and muttered the correct answer and went back to focusing on my own penmanship.

It wasn't the last time Mr. Brown tried to call on me that period, or for the rest of the week. He had definitely noticed my sudden depression and was trying to coax a response out of me, only to receive unenthusiastic replies. It was self-exile, and it was not going to be over until I had forgiven myself.

I packed up my backpack early on that Friday afternoon, my eyes on the second hand of the clock, fingers drumming impatiently on the desk. When the bell finally rang, I leapt up along with the rest of the class, hoping to push my way through the other students and get lost in the shuffle of the hallway. But as soon as I set one foot in the direction of the door, I heard Señor Brown speak behind me, his voice stern.

"Julietta."

I stopped dead in my tracks, knowing full well the unspoken request to talk to me after class that was attached to my name. I watched as my classmates abandoned me to my fate, the door shutting with one final *click*. I dropped my bag and slowly turned to face my teacher, cringing inwardly at the serious look on his face. He tossed his pen on the podium and walked around it, sitting on the desk next to me, eyes now level with mine. "Are..." He started, but shook his head, clearly unhappy with his initial sentence. "What gives, Julietta?"

I sensed his irritation and I shrunk back slightly. "What do you mean?" I asked, playing stupid.

He gestured to me in a frustrated manner. *"This. This silent treatment. You go from being the most participative student in any of my classes to the quietest."* The hands came down to be pressed to the edges of the desk top. "Are you doing okay? Something going on at home, or is someone bothering you here in class?"

Touched by his concerned tone, but unsure of how to breach the subject, I took to staring at my shoes. "Look, Señor, I'm really sorry about bringing up what Señora Barkett said." Closing my eyes, I pushed through my explanation. "It was her personal opinion, not mine, and it wasn't my place to mention it in class. Believe me when I say that I feel absolutely awful."

The room was quiet, the only sounds being the distant yells of students outside in the courtyard. And then came a laugh. From Mr. Brown. "You're still beating yourself up over that?" I lifted my head slightly and peeked over at him. He was leaning over, head tilted to match my angle. "Believe *me*, Julietta, when I say that it's not a problem." As I processed this he leaned back, throwing a quick glance toward the window, watching a stray student run frantically for the buses. His gaze went back to me. "My ego was bruised, sure, but I know a slip of the tongue when I see one." He smiled softly. "There's no harm done. So please, won't you come back to us? Class has been boring without you, and..." He bent over, picking up my backpack. He stood up and handed it to me. "I'm sort of starting to miss your interrogatorios."

I took the proffered bag and flushed.

* * *

ONCE I KNEW THAT MR. Brown was aware of my regret, that he had forgiven me, *and* he was anxious to be on friendly terms with me again, I came back to class on Monday, operating at full capacity. I was relieved, too. I didn't know how long I could have continued in that manner without starting to fall behind in class.

The enthusiasm with which Señor Brown welcomed me back made me feel as if I had never left, and it gave me yet another reason to be continually impressed by him.

Doubling down on hard work and diligence, I was determined to soar to new heights.

As the weeks progressed, my reputation was preceding me. In addition to my obsession with perfection, the unending praise from Mr. Brown served to set me on an unreachable pedestal. Some students either took this as a challenge to rise to the occasion. Still others took it as a reason to despise me even more. Barely concealed murmurs of discontent floated up to me from the back row, but they hardly registered in my ear. I was focused on my teacher. Every compliment from his mouth was an excuse for me to blush, an excuse for me to delve deeper, to feed my compulsion.

Soon after, I came to discover a new side to him.

Mr. Brown was a fan of movies, especially foreign movies. He chose on that particular rainy day to show us a movie from Uruguay, called *Dejame Nunca*. "Clase, this is my favorite movie in the entire world" he said with a grin, wheeling out an ancient television and VCR on a cart from the supply closet.

His favorite movie, eh? Just knowing that piece of information made me eager to watch it. Always hungry for any insight into his soul, I leaned forward in my seat, attentive and excited.

He turned off the overhead lights and popped the VHS into the tape player.

It was the story of a daughter of a rich member of the Blanco Party, Isabel Verela. She fell in love with a poor citizen whose family worked for a Colorado Party-affiliated caudillo during the Uruguayan War of the 1860s. His name was Manuel Fernandes and he saved her purse one day during a pick-pocket attempt. Their worlds collide and passions erupt.

"You can't be seen with me," Manuel pleaded.

Isabel's eyes sparkled in defiance. "Then we won't be seen," she countered.

"What will this mean for us? What will become of us?"

"As long as you love me, I don't care."

Manuel could hold himself back no longer. He swept Isabel off her feet with a searing kiss. My heart fluttered.

Their association was forbidden and they conducted their love affair in secret. Slowly, Isabel's sympathy for the Colorado party grew, and when Isabel's father found out about their affair, the couple decided that they must run away together or else be separated forever. Once their decision was made, they took solace in each other's kisses, every caress growing more fervent, when suddenly...

Something unexpected happened.

Our view of the screen was blocked by something in

Mr. Brown's hand, and he was quickly turning down the volume. The room was plunged into temporary darkness, the only light coming in from the window behind us. Adjusting my eyes, I realized what he was holding was a painting that Sancho had brought in from his art class. Mr. Brown had apparently snatched it up in his haste to get to the front of the classroom. Most of the students, including myself, voiced our disapproval with the disappearance of the screen. Apparently I was not the only one enjoying the movie. "What are you doing?" I cried, looking back and forth between Mr. Brown and the lackluster acrylic painting in mock irritation.

"Well, I wanted to show you Sancho's lovely painting. Look at the trees, clase!" he said, laughing nervously and pointing out the picture, all the while turning a dark shade of red.

When the class's protest grew louder, he made brief eye contact with us before looking away in embarrassment. "I must protect your innocent minds!" he eventually added with a tinge of humor.

Now I understood. This was a racy scene that he was hiding from us. After peeking behind the painting to make sure that the coast was clear, he restored our view of the screen and the classroom clapped in approval. "Finally!" Paco hollered, sticking his thumb and his forefinger in his mouth and whistling. Eventually we quieted down and the movie continued.

The couple had met up in the middle of the night to sneak out of the village and make their way to freedom. Somehow, Isabel's father had followed her to their meeting point, taking them by surprise. He aimed his pistol at Manuel's heart, attempting to kill the young man and drag his daughter back to his estate. At the last moment, Isabel leapt in front of her lover, taking the bullet meant for him in the process. Her father, realizing what he had done, fled the scene in cowardice. Manuel, overcome with grief, picked up the abandoned pistol, committing suicide to join his beloved in paradise. The scene went black on their two unmoving figures, lying side by side. A couple students in the back of the room sniffled.

The movie was not what I originally expected. It was tragic.

Melodramatic.

And it was also the most romantic thing I had ever seen.

This brought questions to my mind. If *this* was Mr. Brown's favorite movie, what kind of romantic was he? What an interesting new puzzle piece I had been given. And what had transpired in the scene that he had censored? I could easily fill in the blanks with my imagination, but that wasn't enough for me. Curiosity had taken its grip, and there was nothing for it but to find it out. I made a mental note to do my research later.

I also couldn't help but make the connection between the fate of the ill-fated couple and my predicament. A student and a teacher? It could only be considered forbidden; the unorthodoxy of it all, the scandal. I barely could keep myself from staring at him the rest of class. My mind ran away with me, conjuring up images of ourselves in that situation, professing our love, running off together... Whenever he turned in my direction, I had to shake myself out my reverie, hoping that he didn't know how to read minds. Or facial expressions at the very least.

When the class was over, I took my time packing my books as usual. I wanted to be the last to leave, to sneak a conversation in with Mr. Brown before the bus left. I pulled out a CD that I had burned for him the night before, looking at my reflection in the silver surface. There was a new album out from a Spanish band I remembered him mention, and I just *had* to give it to him. I hesitated, wondering if my gesture would be seen as a childish thing to do, akin to the much teased mix-tape that so many infatuated lovers had presented to the dismayed crushes. Somehow I saw this as different. Why? I guess I wanted him to see that I was invested in his subject, or maybe that I considered him as a friend. Whatever the actual motivation was, I was going to dive in head-first.

I stood a few feet behind him as he entered information into his computer. It was interesting to watch the muscles of his back work as he typed. However much I would have liked to have gone unnoticed for just a little while longer, I knew he would eventually figure out that I was staring at him. I didn't want my silent observation to come off as creepy, so I cleared my throat to get his attention. He spun around and regarded me, and before he had the chance to question my presence, I handed him the CD. He looked down at it dumbfounded. "What's this?"

I felt myself twitch at the sound of his voice. "Um, I burned a CD for you? I found some new music online the other night, including that one Cuban band that you've been talking about. I didn't know what albums you already had, so I thought you would like a copy." I tried to smile, but on the inside I felt poised to flee, awaiting his inevitable disapproval.

He must had been touched at my offering, nevertheless, because he held the disc up to his eyes, reading the embellished label that I carefully put on the front of it. "Wow. I knew they had made some new stuff but hadn't actually looked for it yet. Thanks, Julietta. I'll be sure to listen to this." He gave me an appreciative smile, which I couldn't help but return.

"You're welcome," I said quietly.

There was a silence, him occupied with opening the lid of the case and inspecting my handwriting, me looking at the laces on my tennis shoes. After a few more seconds passed, I determined that the conversation was probably over. I fidgeted with the straps of my backpack, giving him one last smile. "Well... Adios," I said, and I turned around for the door. But when I had crossed the room and was about to exit, hand resting on the handle, he called out after me.

"Julietta?"

I stopped dead in my tracks, and spun around. What was this? Could it be that he was calling me back? Disbelief and pleasure swirled through me.

"Sí, Señor Brown?" I asked timidly.

My Spanish response switched him into the language, which I didn't mind. I always enjoyed listening to him speak with his accent. "Julietta," he hesitated. "¿Te gusto la película? (Did you like the movie?)

I smiled again to hide my shock. What was I supposed to tell him? That I absolutely loved the movie? That I thought it was the most romantic movie in the world? That I wished that he would sweep me into his arms like Manuel did with Isabel? It took all of my strength to prevent these foolish things from spilling out of my mouth. Instead, I only grinned at him goofily. "Yes, I liked the movie a lot. It was very romantic."

"Good. Good." Another second of silence. He seemed to be in thought, as if he didn't know how to follow up his question.

Noticing his delay, I tried to help by continuing the conversation. "Do you like romance?" My question caused me to cringe inwardly. Was I really asking this?

He blushed a bit. I secretly enjoyed getting that kind of reaction out of him. "Yeah, I do. Have you ever seen *De Libertad y Amor Agridulce*?" He quickly translated the title for me. "Or, *Of Liberty and Bittersweet Love*?"

I shook my head. "No, I haven't."

"Another one of my favorites. I can't show it in class because of..." Here he trailed off briefly, and instinct told me that he was avoiding mentioning more risqué scenes. He changed sentences. "I do believe the book was better."

Aah, books. A subject that didn't get me so nervous. He was already well aware of my penchant for books, I noted with chagrin. I leaned casually against one of his file cabinets, hoping that my act of settling in would encourage a longer conversation. "Yeah, that seems to happen a lot. Have you ever read *Streams Are Less Than Rivers*? I was anxious to see the movie when it came out but was ultimately let down. Important scenes were missing, and the pacing was *so* slow. The book was *so* much better."

He chuckled at an old memory. "You're right, it is. I was actually reading the final chapter when I was supposed to be studying for my college finals." He gestured to me. "Do you know the part where the Surveyor's wife is reading the letter from her dead husband?"

I nodded. It was a very emotional passage.

He continued. "It was getting to me, and I was bawling like a *baby*. My roommate comes in, takes one look at me, and cries 'Brian? What are you *doing*?'" He copied his roommate's horrified expression, waving his hands in front of his face. "Suffice to say, I was a little mortified." He flashed me a small smile.

Brian! So *that* was his first name. After all this time, it felt like a precious gift that had just been dropped in my lap. I wanted to call him by that name; it felt so good sitting on the tip of my tongue. But I decided not to scare him, and I recognized that simply because he mentioned his first name wasn't an invitation to use it. So I just giggled, trying to imagine him crying at the end of a romantic novel. "That must have been awkward." I shifted positions and subjects. "I've always been a fan of well-written stories. In fact, I've been meaning to add to my Spanish collection. Haven't been to the bookstore recently, if you have any recommendations." It felt dangerous bringing up that common link, especially after the last time.

He didn't seem phased. "Oh, so you want my advice now?" He squinted at me, that teasing tone of his reappearing.

"If you're willing to give it, Señor."

"I'll be sure to make a list." He grabbed a pencil off his desk and scribbled something on his planner. He underlined it twice. "Speaking of," he looked back at me, "How's that Marquez working out for you?"

"Like I said before, it's going."

"So not well, then?" He looked triumphant.

I grinned playfully. "I'll never admit to that." I made my way to the door again, taking in the time on the clock.

He laughed outright. "Julietta, Tú eres loca." (You are crazy, Julietta.) My stomach flipped in response to his voice. "Pero me *gusta* loca" (but I *like* crazy). His dark eyes twinkled.

My heart skipped. Under his dedicated gaze, my body felt like collapsing. I couldn't stand it, and the next thing that came out of my mouth was mumbled incoherence. His head tilted, clearly amused at the nonsensical sounds coming out of my mouth. Aware that my face was now visibly flushed, I offered a small "goodbye" and forced my way out into the cold air.

By the time I got to the front of the school, I had missed the bus. I meandered the entire three miles home. The sun was setting by the time I walked in through our front door. Mom was furious. But I didn't care. I was walking on air. He had called me crazy. He had smiled at me with a look of genuine pleasure... I quivered in delight.

His name was echoing throughout my head.

Brian!

seis

"I SAW GRANDMA DOWNTOWN ON my way to school yesterday."

I saw mom shift in her seat uncomfortably from across the table. "Did you say anything to her?" She asked cautiously.

I contemplated her face, how she carried the same shrewd gaze as her gray-haired doppleganger that I spotted through Hayley's windshield. "No, I was only driving past. I made eye contact with her, but I don't know if she recognized me."

"Or ignored you, more like."

"Why don't you just call her, mom?" I saw my dad with his head over his dinner plate, throwing me a warning side glance. I pressed on anyway. "It's been ages and I'm sure she would like to..."

She talked over the top of me. "You should really invite Cadence Atwood over some time, Alyssa. Don't you think she'd make a good friend?"

Grimacing at my mother, I was irritated not only by her avoidance, but also the manner by which she chose to distract me. I huffed. "Cadence Atwood doesn't like me, Mom." I speared a piece of boiled asparagus on my fork. "Besides, she's completely vapid. You don't seriously want me to have friends like that, do you?" I chewed my food, hoping that she would just drop the subject.

"At least she seems to be a fun girl. Unlike your friend, Hayley."

"Leave Hayley alone, Mom."

"You need more friends than just Hayley. You should at least talk to some of the other girls in class."

"I'm not sure how you expect me to be a social butterfly *and* continue to pay attention to my studies."

"Well, if you would just *try*..."

My father, clearing his throat, joined in. "She said to leave it be, hon." I was about to shoot him a look of gratitude when he changed the subject. "Speaking of your studies, how are classes going, 'Lys?"

I wasn't as keen to discuss this subject, either. "Everything is going well. I have that report I have to work on for U.S. History."

Dad set to work on cutting up his piece of overcooked pork, and I could see that he was looking at me out of the corner of his eye. "That's the paper that you stayed after at the school library for, right?" He still didn't seem to believe my explanation for missing the bus that afternoon.

I bent over my food, knowing that any attempt at a lie would show, and I let my hair fall forward to cover my face. "Like I said, Dad." I knew that the true explanation wouldn't go over well. Why would their puritanical daughter purposely spend time alone with a single, male teacher if it was not homework related? I continued shuffling the rice around on my plate until I finally remembered something. "Oh! I finished my application to Berkeley." I said, hoping to distract them. "I should be getting a response by March, if I'm lucky."

Soon the conversation was steered toward my mother's concern about my choice in Berkeley over Stanford and neither of them really noticed that the remaining food on my plate was left uneaten.

The days after, I had Brian on my mind. *Brian*. It felt good to be able to call him that, if only in my inner dialogue. I would think about our last conversation, and about the movie *Dejame Nunca*. Something about that movie intrigued me. Perhaps it was the forbidden nature of the characters' relationship; perhaps it was the attachment Brian had to this particular movie, but the curiosity began to grow within me to a level I could no longer resist. And so the hunt began.

After a futile attempt at searching every video store in the country, I eventually extended the search for the rare film on the internet, scouring the online auctions for days.

I finally found a used copy.

In Bolivia.

The shipping price was astronomical.

Grabbing my debit card from my purse, I found myself hesitating. Was I really going through with this? Was this even healthy, how far I was going to satisfy my obsession? That line of thinking was able to hold its ground for only a few seconds; my emotions overrode my rational questions with little effort. No, I *had* to watch this movie again.

I clicked "buy."

After monitoring the mailbox for another couple weeks to be sure that I was the first to retrieve any packages, it arrived. I grabbed it out of the mailbox and rushed to my room, not wanting to be caught by my parents and questioned about the foreign movie with a steamy cover that I had shipped internationally. I inserted the VHS and pressed play, grateful that my television was ancient enough to still have a VCR. To be safe, I plugged in my headphones to keep my parents hearing what I was watching.

The movie was more emotional for me the second time around. I was alone this time, so I allowed myself to cry, to let my full level of emotion take over me in a way that would have been inappropriate in the middle of the classroom. It wouldn't have been taken well by the other students surely, and I didn't know how I would have reacted should Brian have brought it up. But now I felt free to let it all out: my sadness for Isabel and Manuel's fate, and for mine. In the darkness of my room, I lamented over the hopeless condition I had managed to get myself into.

I finally came upon the scene that Brian had blocked out in class. I was correct in that it was cut out for good reason; Isabel and Manuel were making love, uncensored and in the full throes of passion. No wonder Brian's face was red. My mind ran away with me, imagining me and him...

Breathing deeply, I gripped the edge of my bed tightly. My fingers ached. Attempting to stop that thought process before it even began, I felt like punishing myself for even thinking that way. Allowing this to take root further would only end in heartbreak, I knew, but ultimately my heart was deaf to it. I continued to watch the movie with interest, fantasies blooming and lodging themselves into my mind and my heart. When it was over and I was emotionally wasted, I tucked the video behind the books on my bookshelf, burying it deep, keeping it safe from any prying eyes. This was to be my secret.

It was by pure self-destructive compulsion that I did tell *one* person, though. Brian.

* * *

THE NEXT DAY I HAD managed to convince Hayley into driving us to school so I could arrive early. "So *why* do you need to be here early?" She asked, opening her car door hastily and wincing when it came in contact with the sedan next to us with a dull thud. Hayley was consistently a hazard to herself and others.

I pulled out my bag and slung it over my shoulder. "I want to work on our Civil War paper that's due in a couple weeks. I was going to try and get some research done in the library before the bell." Lies. The paper was finished and already in its neat little folder in my notebook.

Fortunately Hayley was both gullible and uninterested in schoolwork, and her tone immediately sunk into boredom. "Oh, well, I'll just grab some breakfast, then. See you in Rabenstein's class." Without even waiting for my response, she wandered off to the main doors.

Knowing that she wasn't going to bother checking to see if I even went to the library, I settled myself at the entrance, keeping my eye on the staff parking lot. Some weeks ago I had discovered where his assigned parking spot was when I had come in early before. He had pulled up in a tan truck and greeted me warmly on the way in the door. I was hoping to conveniently place myself there and repeat the happy accident so I could have some private time with him before classes.

As time wore on, though, it was apparent to me that his space was going to remain empty. With the first bell ringing, I dejectedly picked up my things and slowly made my way over to my first class.

My bad mood followed me all day, and I wondered if Brian was sick. Was he going to be okay? Who was our substitute going to be? A month ago, a cranky old man had taken his spot when he had the flu. The substitute didn't know a lick of Spanish but was content to stalk down the rows of desks and chastise us if we were not diligently working. I weirdly hoped that it was going to be the same substitute, because if it was, I could spend the entire class writing poetry in Spanish and he wouldn't be able to tell the difference.

By the time the final class came around, I had

resigned myself to the fact that I was not going to be able to see Brian that day. I made my way through the hall and into the courtyard where his classroom was, nose down out of the rain, watching my feet disturb the puddles in the sunken cobblestone.

I was absent mindedly reaching for the handle when the door suddenly flew open, nearly knocking me over. Shocked, I attempted to regain my footing and looked up to see Brian, looking worried and slightly amused at my bad timing.

I was so surprised to see him there that I started babbling, forgetting to censor myself. "Mr. Brown! What are you doing here?! Your truck was gone today."

His look was curious. "I rode my bike in... Are you... stalking my truck or something?"

Oops.

"No, of course not!" My reply was flustered, and I hoped the blush that was starting to creep up my cheeks wasn't noticeable.

His smirk indicated to me that it was, and I ducked past him into the classroom. He waited for me to get by and indicated with a hand motion that he was going out. "Un momentito," he explained, and he went out into the courtyard.

The classroom was empty. Music was playing on his

stereo from the CD I gave him weeks before and I smiled inwardly at the fact that he appreciated my musical offering. I sat on top of my desk and waited quietly, swinging my feet happily.

I saw him come into view outside his window, watching him help a first-year Spanish student who had stopped him with a question about his homework. Brian always called them his "Spanish babies" with affection. I laughed quietly at the memory, all embarrassment from a couple minutes ago now gone.

He came back in and saw me on my desk in the front row, and, having suddenly been reminded of something, he held up one finger and begged my patience once more. I watched and waited as he fished out a slip of paper that was tucked underneath one of his folders. He waved it in the air as he joined me at my desk. "I didn't forget. See?" He handed it over and I received it gingerly with my thumb and forefinger.

Scrawled in his penmanship was a very clean, bullet-pointed list of Spanish novel recommendations. Some of the books listed were also followed by personal notes on preference and suggested reading order. I grinned at him and folded the precious document and tucked it into my back jeans pocket for safe-keeping. I started speaking in Spanish. "Yo compré algo." (I bought something.) I didn't tell him straight away what it was since I wanted him to take my bait and become curious.

My ploy worked and Brian lifted an eyebrow inquisitively. "¿Qué compraste?" (What did you buy?)

I gave him another one of my looks that indicated insanity. "*Dejame Nunca.*"

He paused in surprise, then smiled at me devilishly. "¿En serio? ¿Cómo?" (Seriously? How?)

"Sí, por el internet." (Yes, on the internet.)

He looked at me with astonishment, the edges of his lips curled upwards. I blushed and looked down for a quick second. "Muy bien, Julietta loca." (Very good, crazy Julietta.) Since our conversation several weeks ago, that nickname had become a staple, and I loved it. At that moment, he opened his mouth to say something, but stopped, apparently trying to figure out if he should or not. After a second, he spoke. "¿Tú miraste *toda* la película?" (You watched the *entire* movie?)

I turned a darker shade of red but kept my eye contact with him. "Sí, miré anoche." (Yes, I watched it last night.)

This caused him to flush as well. He started to become uncomfortable and changed the subject. "¿La miraste con tus padres?" (Did you watch it with your parents?)

I blinked in astonishment. I knew what he was trying to do. In a subtle way, he was trying to remind me of my age, perhaps even trying to warn me against discussing this particular subject further. But I simply laughed nervously. "¡No! ¡Por supuesto!" (No! Of course not!) My cheeks burned and I stretched my legs out in front of me, looking down at my shoes.

My reaction humored him and he chuckled. He moved by me, laying his hand briefly on my sleeveless shoulder as he passed. A heat ignited at his touch and shot through my arm. "Julietta..." He said with affection, and he walked to the back of the classroom as the rest of the students in the classes started filing in. I didn't look back at him but raised my hand to feel the spot where he had touched me. I felt my heartbeat pulsing quickly underneath my skin, and I had to catch my breath. I wondered what might happen if he ever absentmindedly touched me again, how I would react...

It was going to be very hard to concentrate in class that day.

siete

THANKSGIVING BREAK CAME AND WENT, and I was happy to find myself back in classes again; I felt stifled by the cold politeness of my extended family and the loud inanity of my peers' chatter was a welcome change. Even Hayley's excitable chatter was a little less grating than usual.

"...I've already got the whole thing planned out, and if I get into the Design Concepts elective for 4th period in January, then I can use the sewing machines in the classroom to finish off the throw pillows. My bedroom set will be so epic! You're planning on signing up too, right? Nothing like an easy A to finish off our last year of high school. And we could work together!"

I shut my locker door and took in her animated face.

I knew that what I was going to say was not what she wanted to hear. "Actually..."

She shook her head violently, already rejecting what I hadn't said. "No!" Her large, fan-shaped earrings swung wildly, and the sound reminded me of wind chimes. "Don't tell me...!"

"Hayley, you know I'm planning on signing up for Advanced Placement Spanish for 4th period."

"You *have* all the foreign language credits you need to get into college! Why risk your precious GPA now?"

I hugged my books closer to my body. "I happen to like Spanish, thank you very much. I've already explained this to you. Besides, I'm thinking of majoring in it now."

Hayley rolled her eyes and started to reply when another voice behind me caught my attention. "Hey, Alyssa!"

The voice was vaguely familiar and I turned to see Patrice Mathers, a fellow senior and in Mrs. Draper's English class with me. Patrice was tall, willowy, with long dark hair and a face with features that always made her look beautiful yet distant and unattainable like a Grecian goddess. She was always nice enough to me, but we usually hung out in different social circles, her in the drama circle and me in the non-existent one. "Hey there, Patrice."

She gave me a courteous smile and plowed into her spiel. "So when we were working in groups today, I remember you mentioning that you don't play any sports, and I was wondering if that means you have some extra time after classes and if you would consider trying out for the Winter musical. We're doing *Bye Bye Birdie*."

"I probably shouldn't. I can't afford to have anything cut into my homework time..."

Patrice cut me off. "Please! We need to fill about 30 roles and we don't even have that many people signed up for auditions! And if you're worried about your grades, don't even worry about it. It doesn't really start to take up too much time until about February. *And* you can count it on your college applications as an extracurricular activity!"

She was really trying hard to sell me on it, her normally stoic face covered in anxiety. I wasn't sure if the anxiety was genuine or part of the pitch. I *had* seen her in productions before, and she was a pretty good actress. I knew that I was going to regret it, but she *did* say extracurricular. "I suppose..."

"Oh thank you!" She threw me off guard by throwing her arms around me and giving me a squeeze. She released me and I tried to find my footing to keep from falling over. She handed me a crumpled flyer that she fished out of her book bag. "The auditions are after class today in the auditorium. Don't worry! If you're nervous about performing in public, you can totally request a role in the chorus. Ciao!" She made a kissy noise, vanishing into the crowd.

* * *

DESPITE NOT BEING PREPARED, I showed up to auditions and made Patrice very happy. She waved at me excitedly from the crowd as I attempted to sing *Think of Me* in front of a crowd and recreate the sample choreography demonstrated by the director.

That was a little less stress-inducing than the fight that I had with my mother later that evening. Despite the solid extracurricular argument, she didn't seem convinced that the high school musical was a good use of my time. Eventually I had to lean on the fact that I had made a promise to Patrice, that I would participate no matter what. I left her in the kitchen to pick on Dad for leaving his contracting paperwork all over the counter tops.

A week later, I received my role: Gloria Rasputin, the sexy secretary. When I finally got a hold of my own copy of the script, I hastily scanned through to find the scene that I was in. The color drained from my face when I read the description on the page.

"I have to do *what?!*"

* * *

WITH DECEMBER NOW IN FULL swing, Christmas was on everyone's minds. The magic of the holiday had worn off with me long ago, and my docket was filled to the brim with last minute essays and rehearsals. But with all the chatter and the good cheer that was enveloping the entire school, my mind inevitably wandered toward the sentimental.

A simple Christmas present. I was sitting on the fence of whether or not I was allowed to buy Mr. Brown one. Was that appropriate? Maybe... No, probably not. I felt it deep in my gut that it was not the best of my ideas when I added a greeting card to the pile of my purchases at the drug store the previous weekend. I tried to make it look like I had placed it there at the last minute as an afterthought, but the older lady that was helping me check out caught the flash of the gold foil on the surface of the card and picked it up to appreciate the design better. "My, what a lovely card. Are you getting it for anyone special?" She smiled at me with her eyes crinkled behind her over-sized bifocals.

Somehow, in that moment, I could only stare at her in horror of the realization of the stupid thing that I had almost done. Really, what was I going to say in that card? Was I somehow going to write something *so* poetic and touching that it would sweep Brian away and he would just *beg* to be with me forever? I slowly pulled the card out of the woman's grasp. "Uhm, actually, I think I won't be getting this card after all."

Now, with only 10 days left, I was sitting in Spanish III chewing absentmindedly on my left thumbnail and trying to figure out my delicate situation. Was there *anything* that I could get him that would let him know that I appreciated him without drawing too much attention from other people and without drawing any concern on Brian's part? I was so completely absorbed in trying to figure out my predicament that I failed to realize that Brian had stopped at my desk. He had noticed my abandoned pencil and exercise questions. "¿Ya estás terminada? (Finished already?)

I had to look directly up to make eye contact with him, he was standing so close. With his figure blocking the light above, he was a set of nearly-black eyes floating in angelic light. I swallowed and removed the tip of my thumb from my mouth, hiding my hands under the table. "Sí."

He laid a hand on my paper, asking non-verbally if it was okay if he checked my work. I simply nodded and let him take it from me. I watched him as he scanned my answers, but after a moment I distracted myself with my notebook to keep myself from staring. After a moment or two, the paper floated back into my vision and landed on the desk with the addition of a couple of red marks on it. "Necesitas usar 'hacerse' en lugar de 'hacer,'pero los demás son correctos. Muy bien." (You need to use 'hacerse' instead of 'hacer,' but the rest is correct. Well done.)

My lack of response seemed to concern him. He bent down into my line of view, and the gesture startled me a bit. "¿Estás okay?" He asked. He was unused to me being so quiet.

I resisted the urge to gape like a fish. "Más o menos. Estoy pensando." (More or less. I'm thinking.)

"¿En qué?" (On what?)

The fact that he was interested in my personal problems filled me with warmth, but I had no idea of how to abstract my words enough to discuss the subject without somehow rousing his suspicion. "Navidad y las problemas que las significa." (Christmas and the problems that come with it.)

He nodded as if he completely understood what I was talking about and stood back up again to check on the other students who were still working. A hand was laid on my shoulder as he passed and it transported me to the moment when he had done the same once before, only without the barrier of a heinously thick sweater. Thinking back on that day and that conversation, an idea suddenly bloomed in my mind that thrilled me so much that when the final bell rung, I was one of the first to be packed up and out the door, breaking my ritual of staying after to have a chat with the Señor.

* * *

THE NEXT DAY WAS WEDNESDAY, the final day before Winter break started. The short week barely felt enough time to accomplish anything important. Many teachers had resorted to busy-work and Christmas activities to fill their final periods. Señor Brown was no exception, and we ended up watching a public broadcasting documentary about Christmas in Mexico. It explained how it was traditional to give gifts not on Christmas itself, which was reserved for religious observance, but on January 6th, Three Kings Day, named after the wise men who visited Christ bearing gold, frankincense, and myrrh. I was easily fascinated by any documentary, even one I had seen before, but some of my fellow classmates were stirring in their seats, impatient to end the class and start their vacations in which they intended to forget for a two-week span that there was ever such a thing as high school.

When the bell rang, I intended to use the commotion to my advantage and set my present unnoticed on the edge of the white board. It seemed best that I didn't draw attention to myself, and even without a card I had a feeling he would know who the present was from anyway.

Intentions and outcomes hardly ever coincide.

"What do you have there, Julietta?" Brian had

caught me mid-placement.

Looking at the unwrapped copy of *Dejame Nunca* in my hand and back up at the puzzled teacher who was wrestling on his winter jacket, I struggled with my words. In the end, all I could manage was a shrug. "Um... Merry Christmas?"

He laughed good-naturedly at my awkwardness and held out his hand as I crossed the room, gripping the VHS as I passed it over to him. "What's this?" he asked although he could clearly see the cover.

I tried to redirect my nervous energy so my voice wouldn't shake, and ended up folding and refolding my hands like they were a complicated origami. "Well, it's not a new copy or anything, in fact it's the one I bought for myself, but it occurred to me that the copy that you have must have been taped ages ago because you can see the frames wobble from playing it too many times..."

"Yeah, I recorded it off of some cable station..." That seemed all he was able to say for quite some time, staring down at the VHS.

Not knowing what to do with the immense silence, I tried to fill it. "I'm sorry it's not a DVD or anything, but it looks like they haven't gotten around to transcrib..."

"No!" He interrupted me, then adjusted his voice when he realized he had responded just a tad too loudly.

"No, this is great, Aly-Julietta." He smiled at me warmly.

I caught his slight slip and it made me beam back in appreciation. I could have stood like that for hours maintaining eye contact with him, adoring the way he was dwarfed in his green snow coat. Speaking of... "Your first winter in the Pacific Northwest. So how are you handling it?"

He chuckled, understanding that I was looking at how poofy he currently was. He set the video down to reach into the pockets of either side of the jacket and show me the thick, insulated gloves that were contained within. "I've been skiing many times before, so I came prepared, but the constant cold temperatures and *no* snow? This is ridiculous!"

I laughed, the nervousness that I initially felt melting away. "Don't worry. You'll get used to Washington eventually."

"Oh, I'm sure I will," he asserted. He grabbed a satchel from near his desk, unbuckling it to place my gift inside. He nodded to the exit, and he switched off the lights as I picked up my things in preparation. We met at the door.

The light outside was soft and muted, filtered by the perennial clouds. I was never one to complain about our weather, and in that moment the silver light seemed to enhance the color of everything in the courtyard. Or perhaps I was simply seeing things in a more optimistic manner because of my present company. I turned back to Brian and was surprised to find him waiting patiently, hand extended. I hesitated, not sure if I was misinterpreting the gesture, but slowly I stretched out my right hand and he grasped it tightly, giving it a little shake. His grip was strong and the heat radiating off him and up my arm conjured images in my head of the blistering sun of California, and oh, God, I needed to breathe.

"Merry Christmas, Julietta." He said quietly.

"Merry Christmas to you too, Señor." I had to focus to push out the words, being entirely too distracted by little facts being tucked into my brain like the one where his hand simultaneously fit yet so completely engulfed mine. "And a Happy New Year, as well."

"Ah, yes," he mused. "It's a whole new year."

The tone of his voice and his penetrating stare suddenly stilled my overactive thoughts. It was so easy to lose myself in those dark eyes, and yet... I let go of his hand and hung on to the straps of my backpack for dear life. "Bye," I said, a bit more hastily than I meant, and made my way to the school's exit.

The next two weeks were going to be marked by an

intolerable restlessness, judging by the daydreams taking hold of my mind as I left that courtyard.

ocho

THE FIRST FEW DAYS OF my winter break were completely hijacked by my mother. My parents, it seemed, were invited to several Christmas parties by a few of her friends who were members of the Lynn Creek Chamber of Commerce. Despite my insistence that I didn't need to go, I was told to 1) put on a smile, 2) put on the dress my mom laid out for me, and 3) get in the car. The parties themselves were seas of endless boredom, with me being paraded around by my mother as her shiny trophy. "She's going to Stanford next year," she would say proudly, keeping her hands on my shoulders to make sure I was standing up straight.

"Is that right?" Random boring adult would ask.

"Apparently." I would sigh, only to receive a pinch to

the back of my arm.

Christmas itself was a fairly uneventful holiday; It was just mom, dad, and myself. The morning was spent in an air of false frivolity. Dad had bought me a hardbound set of the complete works of Sir Arthur Conan Doyle, a gift I had actually wanted. Mom, on the other hand, bought me a file organizer with hanging folders. "What?" she asked upon seeing my perplexed look. She grabbed the wrapping paper from underneath my gift and started smoothing it out and folding it back up. "It'll come in handy for college."

I spent the rest of my break either hanging out with Hayley, who was helping me memorize my lines for *Bye Bye Birdie* or holed away in my room. I was perfectly content to sit cross-legged on my bed and read, Dapper in my lap. There was a renewed interest in tackling *Amor en el Tiempo de Colera,* but even with my dictionary and verb reference, it was extremely slow going. Occasionally, my mom would come in uninvited, claiming that she was gathering my dirty laundry. Really it was an excuse to figure out what I was up to. And when she asked, I would flip my books over and show her the covers, knowing she couldn't make heads or tails of it, and she would leave with another comment on how reclusive I was being.

* * *

IT WAS A RELIEF WHEN Winter break finally came

to an end, and the bus ride to school was absolute torture. I could have gotten there faster had I driven with Hayley, but when the roads became icy I turned her offer down flat, cherishing my health and safety.

There was only one other set of footprints in the frost of the courtyard, and it led in the same direction I was heading. Not wanting to waste any precious time, I hurried my pace. I knew I was going to see him at my usual time at the end of the day, but I didn't know how much longer my patience could hold. I tugged on the bottom of my coat to smooth it out and made sure my ponytail was pulled straight.

I yanked open the door, leaning halfway through the frame. I must have missed Brian by only a few seconds in the hallway, because he was still unraveling the scarf from his neck, back to me.

"Hola!" I called cheerfully.

I saw him start. I was sneakier than I thought. He flipped around, grinning at me. "Hola," he returned, freeing his scarf and setting it to the side.

I took the invitation and crossed the threshold. It didn't seem much warmer in here than it was outside. Clearly the janitors hadn't thought to turn the building's heat back on until that very morning. "So it seems you got your wish," I said.

He tilted his head. He clearly didn't know where this was going. "Excuse me?"

I considered letting him dangle for a bit; his confusion was so cute. I clarified. "It snowed over the break. A whole inch and a half of it. You must be thrilled."

I could see his body relax and he laughed. "Yes, yes. I got my snow. And how was your break?"

I hemmed and hawed. "Oh, you know how it is. I got kidnapped, was forced to jump through hoops in a heinous costume..."

"Corporate Christmas party?"

"Not sure. I think I talked to the mayor at some point, though."

"Ah."

There was a bit of companionable silence. Both of us were all smiles, his aimed at me, mine aimed at my shoes. "So," he spoke up. "What are you doing here so early in the morning? You don't have to be in here till fourth period."

Looking up, I knew his question wasn't accusatory. In fact, the tone was the complete opposite. Brian's entire demeanor seemed to suggest that he was entirely pleased to see me. I felt a fluttering in my chest. "Um, I was just..." I couldn't really think of a reason other than an overwhelming desire to see his face.

"Oh!" he exclaimed, the interruption saving me from the lie I was about to come up with. He went back to his satchel that he left on his desk and fished out a hardcover book, handing it over to me.

I read the title. "Diez Cuentas de Eva Luna."

"Have you read it?"

"No," I replied, flipping through its well-worn pages and perusing the contents.

"Knowing your excellent taste in novels... well, this is practically a modern classic. One of my favorites. I saw it on my shelf at home and it occurred to me that you might like it."

The breath was sucked out of me for a second. "You... You're giving me one of your own books?"

He looked a little sheepish. Shrugging, he scratched the back of his head. "Well, yeah."

I didn't know what to say. The notion that he had been thinking about me while we were away had heat crawling up my neck to the tips of my ears. When I opened my mouth, all that escaped was a squeak, so I settled for hugging the book to my chest, eyes wide with shock.

He laughed. "You're welcome."

I caught my breath, thinking just how stifling my outer layers were becoming. "Oh! Yes. T-thank you."

I looked down at the book in my hands again and closed the few feet between us, leaving only a small gap. I felt myself begin to shake. "I'm just so..." Deep breath. "I mean, this is so thoughtful..." There were more words sitting on the tip of my tongue, but I knew I couldn't say them.

"It would be more useful to you than it would be gathering dust on my shelf." He explained with a small smile. "A book like that deserves some attention from an avid reader like yourself. Someone clever enough to appreciate it."

I choked down the ironic laugh that was threatening to escape. This praise felt intimate, without the familiarity of the classroom fanfare. "I don't know if I'm actually clever or if I just work hard enough to appear that way." The admission surprised even myself in its honesty.

Brian chuckled, reaching out and touching my arm, cradling my elbow. "Learn to take a compliment, Julietta." Looking up at him, his face hovering inches above mine, I took in his sincere eyes. I felt his gentle grip on me as though all those layers weren't hindering us. I thought of that hand, how I had once held it in my own, and I desperately desired to feel its warmth again. *Oh Lord,* his gaze on me was such unbearable divinity...

A gaggle of freshmen burst through the door.

I don't know how long we had been standing that way, but the moment was suddenly broken. It was a split second, but I saw a flicker of what seemed like wide-eyed awareness in Brian's countenance, and suddenly his hand was removed from my arm quicker than had he burned himself. "Pues, nos vemos en clase, Julietta." He took a couple steps back toward his desk.

His sudden change in polarity left me dazed. I looked over my shoulder at the group of freshmen girls and boys who were spilling into the room with loud tales of Christmas vacations. My fingers tightened around the binding of *Diez Cuentas*. A quick shake of my head put my thoughts back on track. "Yeah, I'll see you later, Señor." And I excused myself through the crowd and pushed through the half-open door without any further glance at him. The warning bell rang and I began to run.

* * *

LUCKILY FOR ME MY CLASSES proved to be a distraction from Brian's actions for the majority of the day. With winter break over and only a couple more weeks until the end of first semester, all too many teachers were eager to pour out their assignments.

Turpin handed out a list of terms and concepts that

we were expected to memorize for his big final that was worth forty percent of our grade.

In Draper's class we were handed the rubric for an essay on the major themes of *Othello,* which we were supposed to have finished reading over the break. I had completely forgotten about it, so instead of working on my concept cloud like I was supposed to, I spent the rest of English rushing through Acts IV and V.

Rabenstein was having us take the U.S. citizenship test for her final, and we spent our time answering essay questions on landmark Supreme Court cases, with more to do for homework.

By the time I got to fourth period, I was feeling overwhelmed by my workload, trying to figure out how I was expected to fit all of my studying in and attend rehearsals at the same time. The Spanish classroom was devoid of Señor Brown when I arrived. In fact, he didn't enter the classroom until the very last minute when the bell rang. A voice at the back of my mind whispered that he was trying to avoid me, but I pushed it off to the side in hopes that I was mistaken. His class was as intense as the rest of mine that day, and the majority of the time was spent taking notes on his review of present subjunctive conjugations.

There wasn't a lot of time for discussion, and even though he normally chastised us for packing up before the bell rang, he actually led the charge, collecting his paperwork up in binder clips ahead of time. I wasn't the only one who noticed, and soon everyone else took his example and packed up as well. When the bell rang, we all exited as one mass group. "Adios," he called out to all of us and made a bee-line to the double doors leading to the administrative hallway. I stood in the courtyard and watched his retreat, my inner voice screaming *I told you so.* My time was limited before I was expected in the auditorium, so I attempted to shove my confusion off to the side once again, telling myself that I could ponder it some other time.

Rehearsal proved to be difficult. It was the first time I had performed my scene on stage in front of the group; even without the distractions of the day, my stomach was in knots. The director ended up stopping me several times, her exhaustion with my performance growing with every run.

"Alyssa, I can tell you've memorized the lines, but for the love of God, put some emotion into it!" She shouted from her front row seat, the rest of the cast seated behind her. "You're supposed to be *flirting* with Albert. This guy is your ticket into showbiz!" I looked over at Tim, the gangly junior who was playing Albert. "Remember how you did it back in December? You have to get up close and personal!" She smashed her hands together in an illustrative gesture.

All day, my energy had been wasted with solving the

mystery of Brian's behavior. I was *not* in the mood to flirt. Least of all with Tim. But I took a deep breath and backed up a line. "I do more than just *type...*" I said in the most sensual tone I could muster. I approached my seemingly interested target and pressed into him, one hand on his chest and the other tugging on his pencil-neck tie. "You see, I'd help you out with the secretary stuff..."

Tim, improvising, had decided to reciprocate the physical contact, and his clammy hand reached up and lay hold of the crook in my arm. I involuntarily jerked. Despite the sensation being night and day, I couldn't help but think of when Brian had his hand in almost the exact same spot earlier that day, and something clicked into place in my mental puzzle. The script completely disappeared from my working memory. "Um..."

"Okay, Alyssa, never mind." The director dug her knuckle into her eye socket, most likely from staving off a headache. "We're gonna move on to the next scene and we'll try this again tomorrow. You just go home, drink a glass of water and get some rest, yeah?"

I had already collected my things and was halfway up the aisle by the time the remaining cast stood up. I caught the lilting notes of Patrice's "Feel better, Alyssa!" floating through the air, but I didn't have the capacity to acknowledge her.

My mind was busy entertaining a notion.

Up until then, I had been under the assumption that my moment with Brian was one-sided. That the wave of desire I felt was *mine,* and mine alone. That his gift to me was him being nice, nothing else.

But what if...

What if, his gift meant something *more*?

That the moment where we were standing so close meant something to him as well? That I wasn't alone in feeling that soul-deep ache? Was he avoiding me on purpose this afternoon for that exact reason? Dare I...?

I stepped out into the high school parking lot, my bitter laugh caught and carried away by the chilling January wind. I was kidding myself. This was a hopeless situation, but here I was still grasping at straws and hoping against hope. Making myself miserable like a lovesick fool, reading into every little gesture.

I used to be so level-headed. I used to see reason. Now my entire existence seemed to hang on the meaning of the battered book at the bottom of my backpack. I should have cared about what that meant of my sanity, but instead, I decided to give into it. The fantasy felt so much better than the reality. The freezing gale couldn't touch me.

nueve

SO IT WAS ONLY NATURAL that despite Hayley's best efforts to lure me away to Design class with the promise of an easy A, I was set and bound to my decision to enroll in Advanced Placement Spanish for the new semester at the end of January. I couldn't leave him. I just couldn't.

Taking advantage of every small gesture, every smile I was afforded, I let my dark-eyed muse lead me. I don't know *exactly* when I went insane, when the crazy notions in my head stopped alarming me and started sustaining me. Yet here I was, blind to anything else that a normal teenage girl *should* care about. My life, secretly, was devoted to him. I lived for his class, to see his face and hear his voice for two hours every day on the weekdays.

And when I was at home, he invaded my mind there. It started feeling downright adulterous, even, to give purchase to any other thought but him. It barely even registered anymore that what I was wanting wasn't possible. I was content living with the delusion.

Mr. Brown himself didn't know about the space he occupied in my mind, how much of it he absolutely consumed. He didn't know that every time he came near me, said something complimentary, shared something personal with me in a hushed voice, brushed his hand accidentally against mine, it set off another daydream, another precious moment tucked away in sanctuary.

The only truth that I could hold on to now, the thorn digging deep into my vein, was the very real realization that Brian could *never* look me at me like that, passion in his smoldering, dark brown eyes, and say the one thing that would seal our destiny forever.

I was very well aware of how tragic my behavior would have appeared, should anyone have known; making my situation worse by thinking in this morbid *Romeo and Juliet* fashion, staking my entire happiness on someone who didn't realize how *every* word he spoke had the capacity to elate or destroy me. I was in too deep, I knew. It was only a matter of time before those lines didn't matter to me anymore.

And then came Valentine's Day.

* * *

OUR SCHOOL HAD A LITTLE tradition for Valentine's Day, one that was either looked forward to by those whose had romantic notions or reviled by the type of people who wore black on this particular holiday. During first period, every girl in the school was given a paper heart with their name on it to wear about their necks. It was a giant thing, unavoidable to the eye and hung with a piece of cheap, white string. In between passing periods, girls were not allowed to talk to boys, and if they did, they would have to give their heart to the boy. A tradition of a by-gone era, misogyny at its very finest. But that didn't stop half the girls losing their hearts by the second class, usually on purpose. It was a contest amongst the boys to see who could collect the most paper hearts by the end of the school day. There always was a football jock who was wearing at least twenty about his neck, high-fiving any guy who hooted at him in approval.

By the time lunch rolled around, Hayley was eagerly eying every boy that passed by. She still had her pink heart, name written prettily in large letters, flowers scrawled all over. Despite her best efforts, she hadn't had a guy approach her all morning. It was putting a dent in her ego, and when Zane Mathieson walked by without so much as glancing her direction, she stabbed her baked potato with a fork in frustration.

"They're doing it on purpose!" she whined, looking

at me before turning back to glare at the entire cafeteria. She fingered the string agitatedly.

Instead of my gut reaction of laughing, for her desperation was quite humorous, I nodded my head in agreement.

"I mean, it's not like I'm totally heinous or anything. Would it really be that awful to have my name hanging on their neck?" She grimaced at the thought, and fished under our table for her backpack. She pulled out a small compact and checked to make sure nothing was in between her teeth.

"I still have my heart, too." I reminded her. I pointed at it, cherry red with my name neatly printed in the middle. I wondered if it occurred to her that if *she* still had her heart because no boy could stand the sight of her, then I would be in the same boat, as well.

Apparently it didn't, because she waved me off flippantly with one hand as she tucked her mirror back into its pocket.

"Hayley Gibbons?"

We had failed to notice that a boy had approached our table. Giving him a once over, I determined he wasn't from our class, but, by his appearance, I guessed that he had to have been at least a junior. He was dressed in loose fitting clothes and sported well-worn Converse shoes.

Perhaps he was a skater. Hayley must have known who he was, because she was blushing a deep red. "Hi, Shawn." She said shyly, tucking her long hair behind her ear.

Ah, the infamous Shawn.

"Since you're talking to me, may I have your heart, please?" He held out one hand.

Before I could even blink, Hayley had removed the piece of paper and handed it over to him. "Of course!" she said enthusiastically. She stumbled over her next words. "I... I was kind of hoping you'd come over. I had my heart all morning."

He grinned at her. "I know. I threatened to beat up whoever dared to talk to you before I did."

"Oh... OH!" The realization dawned on Hayley's face.

I suppose Shawn thought he was on a roll, since he turned and noticed my heart in place, as well. "How's it going?" He tested.

I simply gave him a tight lipped smile. He quickly blew me off, though, and gave a little wave to Hayley before rejoining his table of cheering friends on the other side of the cafeteria.

Hayley couldn't keep quiet the rest of the lunch period. She still couldn't believe that for the first time ever, she lost her heart to someone she actually liked. Me, I had never lost my heart to anyone. Not since my first Valentine's Day here at the high school. I played the game well, being very careful and giving the cold stare to any guy who would dare to try mind tricks on me. But this year was different. I kept my guard, waiting till my final class, because I knew exactly who I would give it to.

The rest of my day was spent in anxiety, rushing from third period to my most anticipated class of the day. Even when I finally arrived to the Spanish classroom, it felt like an endless parade of tediousness. In honor of the holiday, every activity was tinged with romance, from writing Spanish Valentine's Day cards to listening to slow Spanish ballads.

As I was putting the final flourishes on one of my cards, drawing an embellished tail on one of the letters, Mr. Brown passed by to check on my work. When I felt his presence, I removed my hand so he could inspect it, watching him nod in approval. As his fingers traced over the poem that I had written, I reveled in his closeness and wished that somehow he would recognize that the words he read were meant only for him.

"Muy bien, Julietta. Sin defectos, como de costumbre." (Very good, Julietta. Flawless, as usual.) He straightened back to his full height, gazing down at me. "From Julietta to her Romeo. A boyfriend, maybe?"

A nervous laugh left me, and I tried to reply, but

speech somehow failed me. I settled for shaking my head.

His smile reached his eyes. "No?" He probed again, apparently enjoying my embarrassed reaction.

"No." I managed to reply, and, to avoid any further conversation in front of other students, I went back to my work.

Finally, after another half an hour, the end of the class rolled around and the bell rang. The other students happily threw their work into backpacks and filed out the class, noisily discussing their Valentine's weekend plans. Brian and I were the only two left. I slowly packed my bag, noticing my little journal, deciding to pull it out. At home, I had abandoned the heavy Marquez novel, admitting defeat. I had spent the weekend rereading one of his lighter novels, instead choosing to translate some of it from English back into Spanish. I flipped through the pages of writing, landing on a passage that was particularly moving.

Cayetano the priest was professing his undying devotion to Sierva Maria, a scene that had reduced me to tears with the sweet misery he felt. Should I? Would he realize what this was? These were not simply translated passages, but hand selected sentiments, a mirror to my psyche.

I hesitated, but my curiosity won out in the end and I decided to take the risk. Without looking at him, just in case eye contact made me lose my nerve, I spoke up. "So I gave myself a bit of extra Spanish homework this weekend, Señor."

By this time he was back at his desk, putting files away. He looked up from his work and considered me. "Not that I'm the least bit surprised, but why do you say that, Julietta loca?"

I handed him my journal, trembling. "So it's not *THE* Marquez novel," He nodded, that teasing glint in his eye sparking, but I was quick to continue before he could break my resolve. "However, I did select my favorite passages in *From Love and Other Demons* and translate them back into Spanish, if you want to give it a glance and tell me what you think." I quickly pointed out which page I was referring to and tucked my hand behind my back to hide its shakiness before he noticed.

"Really?" He said with great interest, looking impressed. I nodded and held my breath. He turned his attention to the page and read through my passages, mouthing the words silently with his lips. I bit my thumbnail as I usually did in his presence, nervous as to what he would think. He got down to the last few lines, stating them out loud as he finished. "*Le confesó que no tenía un instante sin pensar en ella, que cuanto comía y bebía tenía el sabor de ella...*"

A look of recognition passed over his features. "I

heard you quoting this the other day."

My eyes widened in shock. I had been working out the wording alone between assignments yesterday, muttering out the quotes to feel out how they sounded. I must have been louder than I realized. He had actually noticed?

He quickly read over it again, and, realizing there was more, flipped the pages with deft fingers, finding paragraph over paragraph. He read it all, and after a moment of reflection, he finally he let out a little sigh of incredulity. "Wow, Julietta. You are... impressive." He stopped, a question on the tip of his tongue. "...Those were your favorite passages?"

I reddened. So it didn't escape his notice that almost every scene chosen were the passionate ones. I laughed it off and gave him a look of defiance. "¿Y qué hay con eso?" (And what of it?) The challenge spilled out of my mouth with a brazenness that I didn't know I possessed. "No soy una niña pequeña." (I'm not a little girl.)

He chuckled in disquiet. "Sí, Yo sé." (Yes, I know). He trailed off, sensing a change in the conversation.

After taking in his awkward silence, I jumped into action again, afraid to lose to my momentum. "Silly me," I rambled, tapping my forehead as if remembering something. "It's in-between periods, and here I am talking to you!" I took the paper heart off of my neck, smoothing it out delicately before handing it to him. "Here you go." I hoped my tone came off as nonchalant, ignoring the roar of my heartbeat rushing through my ears.

He sputtered for a second, unsure of what to do with the proffered heart. He shyly tried to hand it back to me. "I don't think teachers count, Julietta."

"No!" I cut him off. "I talked to you, and so... My heart is yours. I want you to have it." The idea of him rejecting me shot a pang of panic through my body. I pushed it back in his direction, and he carefully placed it on his desk with uncertainty. He looked back up at me with his penetrating gaze, and for a second I lost my composure. I was certain that everything inside me, all the insecurity, all the longing, poured out between us, and it caught him off guard. I could see the questions forming in his eyes.

Suddenly regretting the line that I crossed, I quickly slipped my mask of friendly student back on and picked up my backpack, slowly making my way to the door. I looked back at him sitting confused at his desk. "Happy Valentine's day, Señor." I mumbled, found my grip on the door, and slipped out.

"Gracias, Julietta." I heard him call after me, muffled by the sound of the shutting door.

I kept walking, the rain of that cloudy afternoon drenching my hair and running into my eyes. I was too busy thinking to notice.

Something was changing between us.

diez

DIEZ CUENTAS DE EVA LUNA was my companion for the whole weekend. Allende had a way of painting scenes in the mind. Brian was right in recommending it. The book was well-loved, and in several places there were pencil scrawls in his handwriting. Some were comments, some underlines of words that he must have had to look up. I laid my hands on the pages and imagined his hands where mine now were. It was as if I could close my eyes and he was right there with me.

When I returned to school the next Monday, it was very hard to concentrate. He didn't make it easy for me, either. As it was, my seat assignment was front and center, my desk pushed up against his podium. At certain times his animated lecture style would cause him to lean over his podium as he spoke, his head hovering above mine. My eyes would trace his jaw line, following his neck down to the shadow of his strong shoulders underneath a white button-up he chose to wear that day. Self-consciously I blushed and pretended to look at something interesting on my desk. His voice was so compelling, though, that I just had to look back up at him. And as soon I would make eye contact with him, see his eyes twinkle with that passion he always seemed to possess, I would falter, and immediately whatever subject he was talking about would be lost to me, replaced by daydreams and a lingering desire to find out if he noticed the way his proximity affected me. It was nearly impossible to listen about present projective verb endings when all I wanted to do was to stare into those dark orbs of his and hear his voice say things I longed to hear.

And they certainly weren't present projective verb endings.

The room fell silent, and my musings stopped abruptly, ended by the change in atmosphere.

"Julietta?" I heard my name being called from the podium. I blinked and came back into focus to see him staring at me, as well as the other members of my class, waiting for my answer.

I shook my head as if to physically scatter my distracted thoughts and attempted to pay attention. "¿Sí?"

I put on my most professional look, shuffling the papers on my desk with purpose.

Brian had noticed me off in wonderland and chuckled audibly, amused with my look of seriousness. "Vamos a formar grupos para leer este artículo" (We are going to form groups to read this article).

I knew what he was telling me, but those eyes of his caught me off guard once again, and the words jumbled together in my brain. "¿Perdón?" (Excuse me?) Giggles erupted from the group of girls in the back, darkly happy with the fact that the star pupil sported a look akin to a gaping fish.

I'm quite sure he was able to see my look of utter embarrassment of not being able to understand the simplest of his phrases. He chuckled again, and indicated with his hands the formation of groups. "Grupos, Julietta. Grupos." I was amazed with his patience with me.

I finally understood, thanks to his sign language. I slowly took out the article that was tucked in my backpack, and moved to join the group I was assigned to. After a few moments, I was able to shake off my dazed disposition and sank back into over-achiever mode, taking charge of reading the passage of *Don Quixote* out loud with translations. My partners, Yolanda and Mateo, didn't object, and they leaned back in their seats and just let me go. They both knew that I was the best at reading and writing in the class. They knew it because of Mr. Brown's constant praise of my work; he had even begun using the essays that I had written as examples of perfect work. With me at the helm, any student in a group of mine needn't do more than simply float along in my wake. In any other class, I would not have tolerated this, but my eagerness to please the Señor won out against any sense of indignation.

I was reading along quickly, finding myself absorbed in the quixotic battle of the *remolino*, when I felt a presence behind me.

I knew darn well who it was, since he always wandered from group to group to make sure we were understanding our assignment. His close proximity always made me sweat and tremble, and this time it was no different. Like clockwork, my heart started pounding. I heard my voice immediately begin to shake, and before I knew it, I stumbled and lost my place in the paragraph. I cursed myself mentally for being so vulnerable.

Why couldn't I speak when he was around?

Wait, that was a stupid question.

I *knew* why I couldn't concentrate.

It was because I was in love with the poor guy and just being near him turned me to a quivering, nervous idiot. I closed my eyes, trying to regroup my thoughts.

Luckily for me, the bell rang at that moment, and he turned to go back to his desk to find his schedule and announce that night's homework. I let out the breath that I had been holding and went back to my desk, glad that I didn't have to think in Spanish anymore for the day, his presence slowly short-circuiting my higher brain functions. As I was packing my bag, I heard a student come in and ask Mr. Brown a question. The voice sounded familiar, and I looked up to see Patrice. She was in one of the lower Spanish classes, and had come in ask about her final grade. He looked through his computer and gave her score. She thanked him and turned to go out the door. I greeted her. "See you at rehearsal!"

"See ya, Alyssa!" Patrice waved and exited the classroom.

There was a moment of quiet and I turned around to see him watching me with an interesting expression. "I didn't know you were in the play," Brian told me.

I smiled, glad that he had decided not to mention my disconnected nature during class. I picked up my backpack and slung it onto my back. "Yeah, I'm mainly in the choir, but I have a bit part where I have to perform a dance solo." A blush crept to my ears just thinking about my routine. "I'm really nervous about it, actually. But it should be good! You really ought to come and see us one night." My hands tensed about the straps on my shoulders, hoping he would accept my invitation.

He nodded, taking it into consideration. "You know, I *was* thinking about going on opening night next Friday."

I smiled in satisfaction. *Perfect.*

He wandered across the room, and I watched as he picked up an eraser and started taking the notes off the board, his back to me. "Actually," he said, "I was planning on taking my girlfriend to go see it."

My heart let out a sickeningly slow *thud.*

A *girlfriend?*

He had a girlfriend... and only *now* he was mentioning her?!

Not that he was obligated to inform me of his private life, not that it was any of my business, but all the same...

I felt like my whole reality was being ripped to pieces right in front of me.

Before I could stop myself, an involuntary cry of shock escaped me with such volume that Mr. Brown flipped around in alarm just in time to watch me stagger. When I saw him starting toward me in concern, I caught myself and made for the exit. I fumbled with the door handle, and when it didn't open, panic rose in me and I frantically kicked at the dented metal.

"Julietta...?" He was almost to me. Frantic like a caged animal, I tried once more with clawing hands. The door finally yielded and I ran out into the rain, leaving behind a bewildered Mr. Brown.

I felt myself giving into anxiety, feeling the tremors take my body over...

* * *

I BLINKED AND I FOUND myself home, not certain of how I got there. All I knew was that I was sopping wet and freezing, water dripping down my hair, dripping from the tips of my fingers. Pervasive like the emotions that were flooding my entire being.

Noticing movement in the corner of my eye, I looked up and realized it was my reflection in the mirror above my dresser. Coming closer, I could see the blotchy red spots under my eyes where tears were spilling out and irritating my skin. Plain face, mousy brown hair. I curled my lip in disgust and self-loathing. How utterly small and young I looked. How *naive*.

What was I thinking?

How could I have possibly believed that I was something that Brian could *ever* want?

How could I have deluded myself so completely?

I curled up into a ball and collapsed onto my bed,

sick to my stomach with pains I had never felt before. Dapper came into the room meowing, somehow aware that I was upset. He leapt up to seat himself beside me, cleaning his paws and providing me with some silent company. I grasped him desperately, closing my eyes and crying silently. Tears covered my face, wetting my pillow, wetting Dapper's black fur.

Why did it hurt so much?

If this is what love felt like, I never wanted to feel it again.

once

IN THE MORNING, I TOLD my mother that I was sick.

"Do you want me to get you anything before I leave for work?" My mother's concerned face and her palm on my forehead made my stomach twist in guilt. But she had never doubted me before, and she didn't doubt me now. It was absolutely true that I was sick.

I was sick of everything.

The reality was that I was in love with a teacher who was 15 years older than me, who had *never* told me that he had felt anything towards me, *and* he had a girlfriend, for god's sake. If he ever really did anything that indicated any feelings towards me, they were muddled and indistinguishable amongst the fantasies. A depression had taken over me, and the truth of my situation left me feeling physically ill. I buried my face in my pillow. "I'll be fine, Mom. I just need to sleep."

Her face screwed up in thought and she checked the time on her watch. She was in a rush to get to work on time. "I think that's a good idea. Get some rest, and call me if you need anything."

So she left me alone in the house while she went about her business.

I called the school, asking for my homework to be sent home. Hayley dropped it off later in the day, appearing at the door with a bunch of questions. I shuffled her off, promising that I would discuss it later, knowing that I would never follow through on it. The next couple days I spent re-reading *Of Love and Other Demons*, letting myself be taken over by emotions and self-pity. I thought of *Dejame Nunca*, and how I could never be like the brave young woman from Uruguay. There was no Manuel secretly pining away for me, waiting for the moment to sweep me away from everything I knew. I was just an imbalanced teenager whose parents came home on Wednesday evening to find their daughter still in her pajamas, still depressed, but supposedly looking much better, according to my mother.

"You need to go to school tomorrow," she insisted.

"But Mom," I complained, using the weakest sounding voice I could muster. "I'm still sick." I even sniffed for good measure.

She simply shook her head, continuing to clean up the kitchen. "You're not sick. You're moping, obviously." Dapper weaved under her feet, begging for leftovers. When Mom tripped, she huffed in an irritated fashion, picking up the cat and moving to toss him out of the back door. Once Dapper was taken care of, she turned and realized that I was still there, my silence only confirming her theory. "Look, if you're having a problem with someone at school, I understand, but I can't have you getting behind in your schoolwork. You'll just have to deal with it."

I thought about continuing my protest, but I realized that if I made a big deal out of it, she would only press me to explain. So it was settled. I was going to school tomorrow.

I'm quite sure if I had told her the real reason why I was moping around the house she would have laughed at me, mocked me. If I told her the way I really felt, what had been going on with her daughter the last six months, she would have become frightened, called a counselor. No, I would never tell her.

I dreaded going back. Going to school would mean I would have to face him again, answer questions I didn't want to answer, be awkward for the rest of the school year. And everybody would notice something different about me, they would know... No. Forget school. I was sorely tempted to just drop out and get my GED.

The next morning I woke up with a headache. My night had been filled with dreams of him. And for the first time, my dreams weren't pleasant. They were of confessions, open secrets. He had turned away from me in those dreams, leaving me out in the cold, or behind a locked door, abandoned and useless. An omen for what I was convinced was going to be a miserable day. I grimly took my shower and got ready for school, deciding the best approach for the day was to set on a mask of indifference. I grabbed a hoodie on the way out of the door, hoping that I would have the ability to become invisible in the folds of the over-sized sweatshirt.

* * *

THE MORNING PASSED QUICKLY, AS did lunch. Hayley was wondering why I was being so unresponsive, and if she actually asked me what was wrong, I didn't notice. The outside world was closed to me. I sunk down in my chair and busied myself with catching up on my physics homework. She finally left me to my own devices, knowing better than to interrupt one of my moods.

When the final period came around, and I walked up to the Spanish door, I stopped, and leaned against the outer wall, out of sight of anyone in the class that might be watching. My heart was in my throat, choking me. My feet were paralyzed. I raked my shaking hand through my hair, hoping it would clear my mind. *Breathe,* I told myself, *just do your work, only speak when called on, then get the hell out of there.* I forced my legs to move and entered the classroom.

I kept my eyes forward and went straight to my desk, pulling out random papers from my backpack, not understanding what I was reading, but poring over it as if it was fascinating. Soft rustling from behind me indicated that he was moving about the classroom, the music that I had given him softly floating around the room. I tried not to notice, not to feel flattered by it. Eventually other students filed into the room and their chattering dulled out the sounds of the stereo. With everyone present and the ring of the bell, it was the beginning of class.

I felt his eyes on me as he greeted the class in his usual manner. Grinding my teeth and looking at my desk, I willed myself not to be lulled by the timbre of his voice again. I had to keep my head clear. I passed forward my homework, listening as the rest of the class discussed the assignment.

Suddenly I heard him asking me what I thought of the assignment. I looked up and regretted it. The entire class was looking at me in a strange fashion. Katalina grinned at me in a particularly wicked fashion between open-mouthed bites of her blue bubblegum. Usually bubbly

Julietta would ramble away in Spanish. Not today. Feeling embarrassed, I willed myself to act normal, but only mumbled something about the assignment being fine and left it at that. I went back to inspecting my desk.

Mr. Brown sighed and sat himself on his stool. "Okay..." The students weren't the only ones who were confused by the change in my behavior. "Now then, I guess we will be practicing our unknown-entity subjunctives. In case you have forgotten since a couple days ago, it's used in sentences like, 'I am looking for a person that is...' They are used in cases to describe something that is not quite certain to exist." He took out a pen and wrote the conjugation for the word ser (to be) on the board in the appropriate forms. Yo sea, tú seas, él sea, nosotros seamos... "So now we will pair up and discuss," He paused for thought, "...what we are looking for in a future partner, starting with the phrase 'Quiero un hombre o muchacha que sea... cualquier.'" He searched around the room and counted up the people. "Hmm... we're missing a person today, so we're odd." He then paired off the students, leaving me for last. "Julietta, you're the odd one out. You're paired with me."

Damn him! Why was he torturing me?

The rest of the students were already getting up and moving to work with their partners, so I sat up and pretended to look at Mr. Brown while he sat down at the desk next to me.

"Entonces, Julietta, ¿Qué quieres en un hombre?" (Well then, Julietta, what do you want in a man?) He asked the question as if it was weighted, as if the answer would somehow give him a clue to my off-putting manner. The question was a magnifying glass, and I was the unfortunate subject of observation.

How cruel of him! What did he want of me?

I felt indignant, and my temper flared up at the unfairness of this question. After a couple of deep breaths, though, I realized there was no point in lying to him. However I chose to answer, I was certain the truth was written plainly across my face. "Quiero un hombre que sea más alto que yo, con pelo moreno y ojos negros. Y quiero un hombre que tenga un sentido de humor, sea simpatico, y tenga una pasión para la cultura y la vida." (I want a man that is taller than me, with brown hair and dark eyes. And I want a man that has a sense of humor, is kind, and has a passion for culture and for life.) *By the way*, I thought sarcastically, *does this sound like anyone familiar?*

He smiled at me. I wanly returned the favor, feeling my previous anger dissipating. It was only then that I realized I had let down my guard. My emotions were plainly in sight. As he looked into my eyes, I let him see what he was looking for. He didn't comment but simply took in what he was being offered. It seemed like an eternity before he nodded, as if to himself, then left the desk and called the class back to attention. I was left perplexed. What was going on?

He gave us some busy work to do, leaving some time for him to work at his desk. The entire time, though, I knew his eyes were on my back. I looked behind to find out what he was doing, just to see him catch himself and pretend to work. He was obviously contemplating something. Questions were piling up in my mind.

The final bell rung, jolting both of us out of our ponderings. My classmates were quick to pile out the door before I was able to get my books in my bag and lose myself in the crowd. Willing my clumsy hands to speed up, I put my jacket on and grabbed my backpack and made a beeline for the exit.

"Julietta...wait."

Curse my slowness!

I stopped abruptly, just inches from the door. I wanted to bolt, but something held me back.

A feeling deep in my gut told me that if I left now, be it for better or worse, I would regret it.

Steeling myself, I turned to face him.

He had stood up, closer to me than a few seconds ago, taking me off guard. He had something on his mind, I could see it in his eyes. His eyes always gave so much of him away. He opened his mouth, and at first there was only hesitation, but finally words came out. "...Is there something that you want to tell me?"

I knew what he meant, but I pretended not to. Fear forced lies to start rolling off my tongue. "Look, I'm sorry that I was so unresponsive in class, it is just that I was tired and..."

"No..."

I could see that he was frustrated, but I couldn't help myself. "...And I was feeling a bit sick yesterday. I did do my homework and..."

"Alyssa!" His loud tone and the use of my real name shocked me and I stopped. He looked at me with such exasperation that for a second I was filled with a strange sadness. He broke eye contact, taking off his glasses and tossing them on his desk. It was as if along with those glasses, he was tossing aside the teacher persona and the inequality that came with it. "I'm not talking about how you behaved in class today, and you know it." He turned back and held out his hand to me in supplication, begging me to say something.

He knew!

My initial reaction was shock. But then again, why wouldn't he know? He was a smart man, and my actions the past few days (past few months, if I was honest with myself), weren't making it terribly difficult to figure out.

This was all too much.

I suddenly felt so stupid.

I never imagined myself in this situation before, and could feel myself descending into survival mode. Perhaps this could all be willed away. Maybe I could convince myself yet that this wasn't happening. This was nothing, nothing at all...

I dropped my bag and curled my arms around myself for protection against some unseen assailant. I looked away from him, not being able to bear the intensity of his gaze. My voice cracked, and with it the rest of my control crumbled away. "Señor..."

In a moment he closed the distance between us and grabbed my shoulders, forcing me to turn towards him. I shuddered under his touch, my breathing coming in short rasps. "Damn it Alyssa...tell me!" He was as much of a wreck as I was; He was gasping, the air between us suddenly stifling.

I gazed up at him, his black eyes glittering with some pain that I had never seen before. I was hurting him, and I couldn't stand it. Silent tears began to fall down my cheeks, dropping off my chin, wetting my neck. I pushed away from him, his grip loosening instantly. Seeking refuge in the corner, and with my back to him, it seemed somewhat easier to say what I felt I must. "I'm so sorry." My voice came quietly. "I didn't mean to... it's just that you were..." I couldn't say anymore as my words became sobs. My head sunk into my hands, not being able to control what I was feeling.

Every inch of me wanted to flee, to tear myself from this wretched situation!

He let out an agonizing sigh. I heard him step closer to me. He saw how I tensed the closer he came to me. He was seeing my reaction. "Alyssa, I need you to tell me truthfully..." There was a long pause where he must have been gathering courage. The wait made me go crazy, but then it came. "How do you...?" He seemed unable to finish the obvious question.

Now came the moment of truth. There was no turning back, no lying. Yet I held back. Something was keeping me back, perhaps the vain wish that this was still just a dream, that I could just wait and I would eventually wake up. But that possibility was shattered as I felt him wrap his arms around me, turning me around once again so I was facing him. No, the racing of my heart, the warmth that came from his body was quite real. This was no dream.

"Julietta..." He whispered. He took his thumb and ever so gently brushed one of my tears away, leaving his hand to rest under my chin, lifting it up so I met his eyes that looked on me with such careful attention.

I trembled, not being able to control myself any

longer. His name bubbled up from me, escaping my lips before I even grasped the idea of what it would mean. "Brian..." There was a convulsive catching of breath at the use of his given name. I sighed with content, happy that I said his name at last. He was no longer Mr. Brown in my mind, but Brian, the man that I loved. Elated at my revelation, I felt myself smile. "Te amo, Brian..."

If my heart didn't burst by the relief that my confession brought, it certainly did when I saw the passion in my heart reflected in his eyes. Eyes that were coming closer, leaning down to meet mine. I felt his breath on me, and my eyelids slid shut, reveling in this closeness, feeling like I was drugged. I felt a longing in his voice that I had never heard before. "Julietta," He murmured. "Te amo."

Euphoria swept over me and my tears started afresh as he lowered his head and our lips met for the first time, electricity shooting through me. My first kiss, and I didn't care if it was my last, if only it would last forever.

I felt my desire increase, the room suddenly unbearably hot. I felt his arms press against my back, his fervor escalating, overcoming mine. I lost the use of my legs and sunk slowly, my back finding the top of a desk, pinned there by the weight of him. I reached up to wrap my arms around his neck, pulling him closer, deepening the kiss, feeling my mouth open, hearing myself moan, as if from a distance.

This was greater than I had ever envisioned.

This was definitely not a dream.

doce

FINALLY, WE BOTH HAD TO come back up for air. As soon as the adrenaline wore off and my vision returned to normal, his smile was there to welcome me back to the real world. My chest heaved up and down, catching my breath. My sense of reality and fantasy was still tipped upside down, intermingling at the back of my mind. Did this kiss really happen?

But the eyes only a few inches from mine were impossible to ignore, twinkling with more happiness I had ever seen in them before. Was I the cause of their happiness? I was so confused.

"Wonderful..." he murmured.

Yes, however surreal this all felt, this definitely all

happened. He helped me sit up and I weakly leaned against him, my strength sapped from me. "Brian..." I just closed my eyes, sighing contentedly.

As if his name was a trigger, he tensed, backing away slowly. Concern seized me when the actuality of the situation started dawning on his face. "*Shit*. Am I really doing this?" he muttered to himself. I waited while he paced agitatedly, pinching his nose between his fingers. The happiness I felt only seconds ago was starting to wane and a dread took its place.

He had made a mistake.

I had made a mistake.

I started wringing my hands with such fervor that soon he noticed and turned back to me. Seeing my despair, suddenly all of the doubt in him was tossed to the side. "Alyssa," He came back and took my hands and held them with both of his.

I looked down between us. How little my hands were compared to his, yet how well they fit together. We sat there for a few minutes in silence, taking in what had just happened. I had no idea what was supposed to happen next. The only thing I had ever concerned myself with up to this point was having Brian return my love. Now that it appeared that I had his full attention, the implications of it suddenly surfaced on the stage of my conscience. Even though I was 18, he was the first man I had ever kissed, and the only man I wanted to kiss. What came after this? My mind was running at a million miles a minute. There were some questions that needed to be answered. "Brian," I braced myself. "We need to..."

He ran a hand down my back, wrapping his arm around my waist and bringing me closer to him. For a second I almost forgot what I wanted to know. I had to cranc my neck up to see him. He was looking down at me, and he knew what I was wanting to ask him. "Go ahead. I won't lie to you, Alyssa."

The way he looked at me in such a serious fashion erased any apprehension that I had. Contrary to the circumstances and beyond reason, I trusted this man completely. I tried to gather my courage. "The other day when you said you had a..." I couldn't finish the sentence, looking down at our hands, our fingers entwined. I squeezed his hand tightly, testing it, still not quite sure what was happening and what wasn't.

He understood what I was trying to ask. "You want to know about Amy, don't you?" Hearing the name of the woman in question made me cringe, even though it was the first time I had heard her name.

"Among other things." I couldn't keep the fear out of my voice and I grimaced.

He saw my reaction and lifted my chin up so I could see him clearly. "Alyssa," He looked up at the ceiling briefly as if he could find the right words floating above our heads. "Amy came around after winter break. She was my attempt to want... to be..." He searched for the word. "She was my attempt to be 'normal.'"

When I didn't respond, he looked down to see me waiting for the explanation, and continued.

"When I met you, I knew there was something different about you, but even so, when I found out you were my student..." He shook his head. "I couldn't even *begin* to allow myself to think of you in any other way than that. And when that began to change, well, I didn't know what to do. It seemed impossible. Even if it *were* possible, I had no idea what I'd do if you felt the same way."

His gaze was suddenly torn away from me as he chose instead to stare off into the nothing over my shoulder. I could see that this openness, this vulnerability, between us was just as unnerving to him as it was to me. He spoke again.

"That's where Amy came in. She only entered the scene about a month ago. The way I felt about you was *scaring* me, and she was a... a desperate attempt to distract myself, to redirect..." After some struggle, he abandoned that train of thought and started again. "Here I was, adamant in clinging to what I thought was normal, persuading myself that it was what I truly wanted. But seeing you just now, looking as miserable as I was feeling on the inside..."

His eyes finally came back to lock with mine, emotion building up rough and raw. "Now that I know this is real, that you are right here, *with* me, I can't live a lie anymore." He brushed his thumb along my jawline.

I blinked, shocked to hear that while I was trying to convince myself that I was alone in my feelings, that I was going insane, he was quietly struggling with the same loneliness. All this time, we were heading down parallel paths, afraid to converge until fate finally forced us to collide. The only appropriate response seemed to be to bow myself to its will in awe.

I started to tear up again, my arms finding themselves around his neck, and I pushed up against him. "You're real too..." came my reply, my voice starting to crack. "And I thought I was the only one dreaming." I stood on my tiptoes and kissed him again with as much passion as I could gather. I felt his hand at the back of my head, entangled in my hair, holding me there pressed close to him. We parted, and he leaned his head forward, our foreheads softly resting against each other. We were able to look into each other's souls; no bars, no hesitance in the way.

"You're beautiful, Alyssa," he murmured.

I blushed and averted my gaze, feeling suddenly self-conscious.

He sighed. "You don't see what I see, Julietta."

I looked at his face, so close to mine. I could see everything. Every freckle that ghosted the bridge of his nose, every line that was ingrained from laughter. He was so handsome, far beyond anything I deserved. *Hermoso.* "Tell me again someday," I said. "Maybe I'll finally believe you."

He smiled softly. "Well then, I'll tell you every day until you do." He gave me another squeeze before taking a step back. "Now for those other questions."

I nodded. "I wasn't prepared for this. What do we do now?" I sank back down to sit on the desk.

Brian balled his fists at his side, looking every bit as lost as I knew I was feeling. "I'm not sure. What I do know is that I'm not willing to mess this up. We have to be careful." For good measure, he backed up another couple of steps. "We should take this slow. Nothing could ruin this faster than letting our passions," Inhale. Exhale. "get the better of us."

I couldn't help but grin at his expression, but inside I was deeply impressed at his grand gesture. "I want to see you somewhere," I impulsively told him. "Somewhere away from here." I indicated the classroom with a roll of my eyes. "I mean, maps of Centroamérica y El Caribe are well and good, but they don't make for the most romantic atmosphere, don't you think?"

He laughed. "¡Oye! Don't knock my decorating skills. Besides, I don't think it's so bad. After all, I fell in love with you in this room, Julietta loca." He grinned wildly at me, and before I could brace myself, he took two strides and I was swept into the air, carried by Brian in his arms over to the door, and he set me down with my feet planted firmly on the mat.

I regained my bearings, laughing, recognizing along with him that I needed to leave before people started to miss us. I picked up my backpack and fished out a ballpoint pen and the first paper that I could get a hold of. He knew what it was for, taking it from my hand and quickly writing his number on it. I watched him as he wrote in his slanted handwriting:

-De Brian a su Alyssa-

So I was *his* Alyssa now? What a great feeling.

He handed the paper to me, which I folded neatly and held to my lips in reverence before I tucked it carefully into my pocket. He bent down to kiss me on my cheek. It burned under his touch. I wondered idly if it would always feel like that, if even the slightest contact would sear into my memory forever. He leaned in close to me. "Llamame, Julietta." (Call me, Julietta)

I shivered. I couldn't hold back the joy I was feeling. "Nothing could stop me from calling you, Brian." I slipped my backpack on and opened the door with ease; anxiety could have its grip on me no longer. "I'll see you tomorrow in class, Señor Brown," I said in an amused tone.

He laughed at me. "Just try not to lose concentration tomorrow, Julietta loca." He gave me a mischievous look.

"It's going to be hard, mi amor," I said with a laugh.

His smile faded into emotion. "I love you."

It sounded just as nice in English as it did in Spanish. "And I love you more." I replied, wanting to run back into the room and embrace him again. I consigned myself to blowing him a kiss, and forced myself out the door.

He probably heard me break out loudly in song in the middle of the deserted courtyard the moment the door closed. And I wanted him to hear me. He brought me so much happiness.

Brian loved me!

trece

LUMINESCENT, FIVE-POINTED STARS FORMED CONSTELLATIONS over my head, a remnant of my short-lived fascination with astronomy and Galileo in freshman year. My eyes sought out Polaris from the faux Big Dipper and I tried to control my breathing. Mom and Dad had already retired for the night in their bedroom on the other side of the house, and after spending a disproportionate amount of time preparing myself for bed and delaying the inevitable, I was lying face up on top of my comforter, gripping my cell phone uncertainly and making a wish on my North Star.

With the adrenaline of the afternoon now faded, I doubted. It didn't matter how many times it had been proven otherwise; what if somehow this was still all in my imagination? What if I called this number and it turns out I was mistaken? My logic told me that this was a ridiculous line of thinking, that I had to trust my senses and to stop gas-lighting myself. But as it was, in the dark of my own bedroom, surrounded by the organized piles of my teenage life, I felt very small and childish.

I exhaled, thought *to hell with it*, and hit "Call."

An eternity passed, a seemingly infinite number of dial tones.

Click.

"Hello?"

I hesitated. "Hello." My voice was quiet and small.

"¿Cómo estás, Julietta?" His voice was warm, his pleasure at finding me on the other end of the line evident.

And suddenly everything was perfect.

"I'm wonderful," I replied, smiling widely even though I knew he couldn't see. "You wouldn't *believe* what happened to me today."

"I have an idea." He chuckled. "Everything is falling into place now. This afternoon, for instance, as soon as I left the school, I had a talk with Amy."

"How did she take it?" I didn't even know this woman, but I felt guilty as hell that she was experiencing a breakup because of me and my stupid feelings.

Brian could hear the concern in my voice. "You know what? She was fine with it. She had been feeling as if we were drifting apart anyway, so everything is copacetic." A pause followed by a slow exhale. "Are you just as... *euphoric* as I am right now, Alyssa?"

"That this is actually happening? That I am properly allowed to call you *Brian* now? Yes, I definitely am."

A comfortable silence settled between us for a moment, and I relished just hearing the sound of his breathing through the ear piece. I closed my eyes, and my imagination filled the gap; he was lying next to me in this welcoming dark. "So, what were you up to before I called you? Not sleeping, I hope."

"Sleeping? No. I was actually doing some prep work for second period next week. But you're more than a welcome distraction." I heard the rustling of papers as he set them down on some nearby surface. "Do you want to know when I first knew?"

"Knew what?"

"That you were different, that you meant something more to me?" His voice was hushed, reverent.

It occurred to me just then that something had been uncorked, let loose in him that afternoon, and for all the time that had been wasted, he was aching to catch up. He was tearing at the wall that had separated us and making everything transparent. I shuddered. "When was it?" My tone matched his.

"You had already piqued my interest at the store that day. You were so... delightfully stubborn." I could hear the fond smile. He continued. "That fascination was always my downfall. It was like a spark that I kept trying to extinguish. But then you would come into my class every day and whatever new thing you had to say would set it sparking again. And that day, right before winter break, you took my hand, and... I can't explain it, but in that moment I felt I found my kindred spirit, and as soon as I realized that, there was no extinguishing the fire ever again..." He trailed off, and I had no way to respond, blushing madly in the dark, trying to stave off tears. Luckily something must have occurred to him, because there was an exclamation of *oh!* followed by "I have half a dozen questions for you."

I welcomed the change. "Really?"

"It wouldn't have been appropriate of me before, but I've been dying to turn the tables on you for some time now."

It only took a second for me to register what he was wanting. I sat up in excitement. "Am I going to go through my very own *interrogatorio*?"

"I won't be as relentless as you, I promise," He teased.

"Aaw, that's low. I couldn't help it if I found you utterly captivating."

"Yeah, that was obvious."

"Really?"

"Really."

Here I was thinking that I had managed to hide myself well, and it made me feel slightly embarrassed that my heart had been on my sleeve this whole time. "I'll have to work on that," I responded, making the mental note. "Okay. Go ahead. Ask away."

"Do you have any siblings?"

I sighed. "No. Sadly, I'm the product of two older parents who wanted one perfect *wunderkind...* Why? Do you have any siblings?"

"Yes, but I'll get to that later. ¿Me toca a mí, recuerdas? This is *my* interrogatorio."

I smirked at his playfulness. "Sorry." It was a poor apology given my mischievous air. "Please. Continue."

"So no siblings. Any family? Cousins nearby, perhaps?"

"All of my dad's family is back east in Massachusetts. We moved here when I was four, and only my grandma is nearby."

"Are you and your grandma close?"

"...No." My answer was sluggish. "There was a... fight, a fallout, between her and my mom about ten years back. She lives only a few miles from us and I'm not allowed to talk to her."

There wasn't a response initially. "Do you miss her?"

"Sometimes," I admitted. "I mean, I see her every once in a while around town, but it's like she sees my mother instead of me."

A large exhale of breath on the other end. "Damn."

"Yeah," I agreed.

"You've been in Washington since you were four? In Lynn Creek the entire time?"

"Pretty much."

"So," and here I could tell that he was trying to lighten the mood. "What was Alyssa like as a little kid, hmm? I can imagine that inquisitive mind of yours got you in trouble quite a bit."

"I was a bit of a bossy one, as well." I asserted,

smirking at a few old memories. "Here's a story for you: I was friends with Emily Stravinski and Helena Smith once upon a time. Then they hit middle school and decided that cheerleading and makeup were the latest and greatest. I was of the opposite opinion, and we went our separate ways..."

Brian interrupted. "Wait, Stravinski and Smith?" He mumbled to himself as if he was trying to place the names. "Aah." He recognized them now. "All in all, I think that that particular parting was for the best."

"Agreed."

"Continue."

"Emily, Helena, and I used to play together every day together and, well..."

"Yes?"

"I would hole them up in my old basement. I had stored up old textbooks that my dad would find for me, and I would force them to play school. And I was the teacher. *Every* time."

I heard him sputter. "Are you serious?"

"Fake report cards and everything." I shrugged. "I've kind of always wanted to be a teacher, so..."

This was apparently so funny to Brian that his

phone had to be put down while he laughed loudly for a solid minute. Finally, I was picked back up.

I tapped my index finger in mock impatience against the side of my cell. "You find that funny, hmm?"

"Hilarious *and* ironic, yes."

"Can it be my turn now?"

"Por supuesto, Julietta. Te toca a tí. The floor is yours."

"You said you had siblings."

"One. I have a younger sister, Michelle. She's five years younger than me."

"And she's living down in California?"

"San Consuelo, yeah. That's where I moved from."

"What's she like?"

"She's the sweetest person you'll ever meet." The affection in his voice was evident. "Always goes out of her way to make you smile. You'd love her. We were thick as thieves growing up. She's married now, just had her first baby last year."

"So you're an uncle now, huh?"

"Yep," He answered proudly.

The mention that his younger sister was a married woman with a baby reminded me of the fact that I was indeed involving myself with someone who had already been living in the adult world for quite some time. Inadequacy felt like it was creeping up my throat.

"You still there, Alyssa?" Brian asked.

I shook my head. "Of course I am." Hearing his concerned voice in my ear forced me to remember also that the way in which Brian and I interacted was so natural that it bridged the age gap. That awkwardness would only be there if I let it. So I swallowed the aversive sensation down and tried to ignore the self-abasing voice in my head. "The rest of your family is down there, too?"

"My mom lives in San Consuelo too."

"Just your mom? Sorry if I'm prying too much..."

"No, it's fine." He assured me. "Not much family besides my mom anymore. My maternal grandparents died about 30 years back and my father left when I was six years old."

"Oh," I said softly.

My response must have told him that I didn't necessarily know how to ask the follow-up question, so he volunteered the information. "My mom did the best she could, you know? But 'Chelle was only a baby and we didn't really have family to fall back on. My mother was shuttling between jobs and when I wasn't attending school I was always in some type of daycare."

"It must have been hard." It was the only thing I could think of to say.

"It got better as we grew up. I only transferred three times in high school."

"*Only* three times?!" It was hard enough for me to establish my personal niche at Lynn Creek High School, and I couldn't imagine having to repeat that experience three times over. Suddenly I found myself trying to envision a younger Brian Brown in my mind. "What were you like in high school, anyway?"

"Fairly invisible, really. What with all the moving, it seemed best to just keep my head down, not draw attention to myself. Every time I transferred, I'd have to either relearn a subject or I would be left out of the loop altogether, so I just gave up on getting good grades. I wasn't as driven as you are, Julietta. Things stabilized in junior and senior year, though, and there was one teacher, Mr. Moore, that came alongside me and reminded me of my own middle-school desire to teach Spanish. He encouraged me to reapply myself to my studies. Ended up being a father figure when I didn't have one."

I let that information sink in for a little bit. "Do you... did you ever reconnect with your dad? I mean, you don't have to talk about it if you don't want to..."

"No! I want to. It's good to talk about these things," Brian said, and I nodded to myself in recognition of this truth. He continued. "Other than the sporadic child support check when I was younger, I haven't heard from him since. Michelle doesn't even know what he looks like, and Mom tossed or mangled any photos that contained him."

"Are you still angry with him for what he did to your family?"

"Not anymore. But when I was little, I really, *really* was. I remember this one time when I was seven. I wanted to learn how to ride a two-wheel bike, but my mom never had the time to show me. All the neighbor kids were making fun of me, you know how it is."

"Yeah, I do."

"One weekend, I decided enough was enough, and I pried the training wheels off my bike with a wrench I found and I was going to teach *myself*. My Mom was in the house tending to Michelle since she was running a high fever, so I went out into the driveway to practice, and, well, to cut a long story short, I fell. Hard. I broke my arm on the edge of the curb, and I could do nothing but lie there on the ground and cry. It took my Mom nearly 20 minutes to find me, and by the time she did, there was only one thought running through my head over and over: 'If my Dad were here, this never would have happened.'"

That was when the real silence settled in. The cell phone in my hand was being held firmly against my ear, but I held my breath for fear of disturbing this great, all-revealing quiet. The instant trust that was being granted and the enormity of what Brian was sharing with me held me captive. Feeling both privileged and humbled, I finally felt pressed to break the silence. "Thank you *so* much for sharing with me."

"You are most sincerely welcome." And by the way he said it, I knew that sincerity was a promise of so many shared things to come.

The moment, however, was ruined by a black mass of fur that pushed open the crack in my door. It ran full-tilt toward my bed, making a leap that had it landing square on my stomach. "*Uf!*... Dapper!"

Brian was confused. "Dapper?"

I gave an explanation. "Dapper is my cat, who apparently just decided to inform me that it is time for me to be in bed."

"You're a cat-person?"

"Yes, I am."

"Good to know, good to know."

"Is that a problem?"

"Ooh, I don't know. There are *so* many things I like about you, but I don't know if I can handle the whole cat-person thing." He was clearly joking, the mood returning to a less somber one.

I tried to sound disappointed. "Well, I guess our relationship is doomed, then." As a mock-aside to myself, I muttered, "*Damn,* that was short."

He laughed again, and it made me glad that he appreciated my sense of humor. "Well, we should both be getting to sleep. We still have Friday tomorrow, and we'll need to be as composed and guarded as possible."

Thinking of the challenges that we would have to face together threatened to destabilize my good mood, but the key part of it was we *were* together, and that was worth all the challenges in the world to me. "We'll be on our best behavior, won't we, Señor?"

"Claro que sí, Julietta. And I have one more question for you. Not a serious question, but you can sleep on it and ponder over it all day tomorrow."

"Shoot."

"If you could travel anywhere in the world, where would you begin? I'll start you off by highly recommending Spain. Moorish architecture, fantastic art museums, but, of course, you know I'm biased."

I giggled. "Claro que sí."

"Te amo."

I didn't know if I would ever get used to hearing that. A shiver crept up my spine. "Y yo a tí."

"Goodnight, Alyssa."

"Goodnight, Brian."

Click.

catorce

THE NEXT DAY, I TRIED my best to keep a straight face during class. And so did he. If anyone was aware of my drastic change in behavior, that I no longer averted my eyes from his gaze, that I couldn't stop smiling, I didn't notice. I was in bliss. That we had to be cautious was something that we in theory both understood and appreciated, but in practice it was difficult to pull off when we were in each other's presence. We spent the period secretly flirting each other, glancing over our shoulders to catch a glimpse of one another as one passed, purposely letting our eyes linger until the other one turned around, at which point the culprit would pretend as if the lesson was thoroughly absorbing. It became a game.

An hour passed in this manner, and near the end of this excruciating length of time, Brian handed back our corrected tests from a week ago. Most students were already packing their bags by this time, discussing weekend plans (which most likely did not involve homework), and they hastily stuffed the papers in amongst their binders. I looked over my test and appreciated the 'A' on the front, but upon flipping over to the back page, I found a note in his handwriting:

I can't wait for this class to be over, Alyssa. I can't stand being right in front of you and having to put on an act.

When I saw this, I broke out in a giggle, which brought a smile from Brian, but odd looks from my classmates. Why would anyone think their test was amusing? I blushed lightly and tucked the test into my notebook.

It was the last period before the weekend began, and after what seemed like an eternity, the bell finally rang and I pretended to be busy working on something while the others packed up and filed out of the classroom. Everyone had apparently gotten used to my overachieving presence and so the sight of me continuing past the bell on a Friday afternoon surprised no one. I looked up to see Brian erasing the board, a grin on his face that probably matched mine. I could hear students passing through the hallways, lockers opening, footsteps fading.

After a few minutes, everything finally fell silent. Thank goodness the classroom was off the beaten path. Sensing that the coast was clear, I spoke up, directing my comment at his back. "You know, I usually pride myself on acing every test I'm given, but I would say that on the test of 'keeping a poker face,' we failed pretty horribly."

He set down the eraser. "I'm not sure where you're getting this 'we.' I clearly passed. You, however, *Julietta*, receive a big, fat F."

There was only a moment's pause before we both broke out into laughter. He flipped around and met my gaze, and I saw that his defenses had dropped, both of us losing the thin disguises that we had been wearing all day. I dropped the pencil from my hand and stood up, rushing over to him, feeling him embrace me. I buried my face in his scent, feeling his hand cup my chin, lifting it up so he could kiss me. The kiss was sweet, passionate, making my stomach churn in desire. My eyelashes fluttered open and I looked full on his face, completely content.

"Hello, there," I said demurely.

He treated me with a warm smile. "Hello."

I leaned into him and tucked my head underneath his chin. "Somehow this reminds me of something we did yesterday."

He chuckled and tightened his grip around me.

"Julietta loca," he said endearingly.

I started to shift into a more comfortable position, but he bent his knees and down we slid against the wall, settling on the floor. I twisted so my back was against his chest, and the feel of his heartbeat so close to mine stopped my thought processes. All I wanted to do was to revel in our closeness, but eventually I picked up where we left off on our phone conversation from the night before. "So I thought about your question, you know, about traveling, and I slept on it. To be honest, however much I would *love* to visit Spain, I would have to say Italy comes first on my list. There's enough history there to fill me to the brim so I can die happy." I held my hands out in front of me for emphasis and I smiled dreamily.

I felt him chuckle behind me. "I can't deny the appeal of Italy. It's beautiful there, and the women? *Muy* caliente."

I elbowed him and he laughed. I continued, sighing. "You're so lucky that you've been to so many places. I'm practically itching to get out of this town. There's so much world and so little time."

Brian leaned his head forward, nestling his chin in my neck, his mouth near my ear. A shiver went down my spine, and I could feel his lips curve into a smile. He was definitely enjoying getting such reactions from me. "I've had some time to go to those places. But I wasn't with you then. When your itch fully manifests and it pulls you to the four corners of the world, you won't be alone. No te preocupes (Don't worry.)"

Pleasure rose up within me at the insinuation in his statement. I turned and pressed a kiss to his temple. "You know, Señor, that itch will have to wait. I'm expecting to receive my acceptance letter from Berkley any day now. First Berkley, *then* the world."

Brian grunted in faux-annoyance and leaned back against the wall. "Ah, yes. College. Don't remind me." His quietness indicated to me that he was thinking about the fact that at the end of the summer, I would be packing up and moving off. It was too early for me to say, but how would our relationship withstand the distance? "Maybe I can follow you," he mumbled, and I realized he was asking himself the same question.

I reached down and patted him reassuringly on his leg. "We'll cross that bridge when we get there," I said. "No te preocupes." I smiled back at him, and changed the subject. "I have to leave soon. We're starting up our final dress rehearsals for the musical. I won't be able to have a lot of time next week. You're still thinking about coming next Friday night for the opening?"

"I wouldn't miss it for the world," he replied. "Although, don't expect me to be handing you any roses in the foyer. That would be a tad too transparent."

"Agreed."

"You'll just have to wait until after," he added gleefully.

My mood sobered, still in awe of how much my situation had changed in less than 24 hours. "Flowers from someone *other* than a family member on my birthday," I mused quietly. "Don't think that's ever happened to me before."

The look on his face was unreadable. "That's a shame, Alyssa, because I can't think of a woman more worthy of them than you." He brushed a thumb across the apple of my cheek.

Woman? I blushed, feeling undeserving of the compliment.

"Well, then." He braced himself and got back to his feet, holding out his hand and helping me up as well. "I should let you go." He tugged at the corners of his button-up shirt.

I angled toward him and he embraced me once again. "I'll call you when we get out."

He smiled and bent down to kiss me on my forehead. "I can't wait. In the meantime, I have to finish corrections on some Spanish One assignments. And *you* better not forget to work on your ensayo (essay) this weekend. You may be busy with the play and with your new boyfriend,

Julietta, but I'm not going to take it easy on you!" He gave me a stern look, and his arched eyebrow made me laugh.

I tried hard to put on my most serious tone, but failed. "Yes, sir." I gathered up my books and the pencil that was dropped and forgotten on the floor, feeling his eyes on me. I welcomed his gaze now, feeling more comfortable with his eyes on me now than without them.

I slowly made my way to the door, not wanting to leave. I leaned against the door frame, watching him watching me. It was just one of those moments where the silence was so impregnating that I felt I had to say something, and suddenly the words just slipped off my tongue, poetry spilling out of my mouth like water:

"En el abismo (In the abyss)

Te sigo (I follow you)

Estás conduciendome (You are leading me)

con tu voz (with your voice)

Y miradas pasajeras (and passing glances)

Sabes que no puedo vivir (You know that I can't live)

Si solamente supieras (If only you knew)

que no puedo respirar... (that I can't breathe...)

Sin ti." (Without you)

"...No puedo respirar...sin ti." He finished with me, giving a devilish expression, waiting for my reaction.

My mouth fell open in amazement. "You!" I laughed, jokingly pointing an accusing finger at him. "And here I was thinking I was *so* clever for discovering Carmen Marín all by myself!" I flushed a deep red.

He grinned even wider. "And you did. But next time you hand in your folder for a work check, make sure you remove your journal of translated poetry, Julietta." He looked down for a moment, changing the mood. "But you did hand-pick some beautiful sentiments."

My smiled slowly faded, feeling that my emotions might take me over. "They were meant for you, Brian. All of them were."

He pierced me from across the room with that look that made me want to run over to him and kiss him once again. "Yo sabía," (I knew,) he replied quietly. "Y gracias." (And thank you.)

I smiled delicately, and blew him a kiss. "Te amo." I whispered before I backed out of the door.

I set out at a quick pace, realizing that it was getting late, and headed out to the auditorium on the other side of campus. My head was still swirling with our conversation, and yet I already couldn't wait to call him that night and hear his voice again.

quince

BY THE TIME NEXT FRIDAY rolled around, we had become much more adept at handling ourselves in public.

By the time next Friday had rolled around, we considered ourselves *professionals*.

The bell rang, and I slid into my seat with an air of composure. Pedro and Yolanda burst into the room at the last minute, discussing what, I'm not sure, but it had something to do with Pedro's amazing athletic skills. Adding that to the continued conversation amongst the other students, and the entire classroom was a noise-filled chaos. I was the silent eye in the middle of the storm.

Brian passed to the front of the classroom, and as he passed the air was stirred up with the hint of familiar aftershave. I closed my eyes for a brief second to catalog the scent and regained my surroundings quickly. I watched as he set a pile of transparencies on the podium and place the first on the projector. His reading glasses, making a welcomed appearance, were perched on the bridge of his nose, and as he looked up to scan the class for any absentees, his eyes settled on me. I could see the corner of his mouth twitch before he asked casually, "¿Has completado tu tarea, Julietta?" (Have you completed your homework, Julietta?)

I pursed my lips, holding back a rather coquettish answer. I knew that his question was being used as a placeholder for the more personal greeting, so I followed suit with my own placeholder. "Claro que sí, Señor." (Obviously, Señor.) *I miss you too, Brian,* I thought.

Before Brian could reply, Pedro blundered into our little discourse, overhearing the subject. "Aw, shit! I knew I forgot something! Señor Brown, I promise I'll turn it in on Monday!"

Rolling his eyes dramatically, Brian leaned forward towards Pedro, cupping a hand over one ear. "¿Inglés? Lo siento, pero solo comprendo el español." (English? I'm sorry, I only understand Spanish.) He raised his voice to address the rest of the class. "¡Silencio! ¡Empieza la clase! Pasen su tarea al frente, por favor." The class was suddenly silent as people started rummaging through bags and papers slowly trickled up towards the front rows.

After the planned lecture on circumlocution and ways to talk around a word in Spanish that you may not know, the rest of the period was spent in pairs while we practiced our circumlocution skills through debate. Whether for his education or his punishment, I'm not sure, Brian paired Pedro with me.

I won the debate.

Class ended, and not much time was spent after the bell with Brian. When the coast was clear, I pressed a quick kiss to his cheek as he sat at his desk filing away his notes. He instinctively turned his head to kiss me back properly, but I simply grinned at his frustration and stood back up, slinging my backpack over my shoulder. "You can save that for after my performance tonight."

He looked up at me from his seat and let out a long-suffering sigh, but its effect was spoiled by his lop-sided smile. "I suppose I must."

I backed up to the door. "I'm skipping out on the after-party, so if you wait up after the performance, I'll come find you." He stood up, stretching his arms over his head. The hem of his shirt rode up and a small section of his stomach became exposed, revealing the top of a pair of green boxers. Without any awareness of tact, my head involuntarily tilted sideways to better my view. Brian noticed where my attention was directed and lowered his arms, and a hint of red passed through his cheeks so quickly that I almost didn't notice it. Once I realized I was staring, however, I shook my head to correct myself. "I'll see you after, Brian."

He chuckled and I made eye contact with him once again. "I'll be waiting."

"Wish me luck."

"¡Mucha mierda!"

I blinked, a little confused. "I'm sorry, but did you just say 'A lot of shit?'"

He laughed and waved away my concern. "It's just what they say. You know, the whole 'break a leg' thing."

"Ah." And before the enticing glint of humor in his eyes lured me into being late, I forced myself through the door and towards home.

* * *

I ONLY HAD A SMALL space of time to eat an early dinner and gather my stage makeup before I had to rush back to the school auditorium.

To say that the backstage was a flurry of anxiety was an understatement. Stagehands were hurriedly trying to locate all of the props in time for curtain call. A gaggle of freshman who represented the majority of the chorus were all practicing their harmonies before the music director pulled us to the choir room for one last rehearsal before the curtain rose. I headed over to the dressing room while I still had the chance, slipping on my costume. I grimaced at the 4-inch heels and my bare stomach in the mirror, feeling uncomfortable with the amount of skin that was showing, knowing that it was necessary for my role. The blonde wig was slipped on and my alter-persona was complete: Gloria Rasputin, the seductive secretary in *Bye Bye Birdie*. As I took in my character, I tried to figure out why I ever thought it was a good idea to be in the musical in the first place. I should have never listened to Patrice when she came recruiting for the high school musical. No amount of extracurricular credit was worth this humiliation. I had no idea how to be seductive, and now it was going to be obvious to an entire audience. An audience that contained my parents and Brian. I felt a little sick to my stomach.

Once the curtain was raised, however, everything was a bit of a blur. Act One seemed to pass in the blink of an eye. The second act came before I knew it; the intermission did not even register to my overworked nerves. Within minutes I was on stage, flirting my guts out, tugging on the tie of "Clammy-Hands" Tim, and stomping out a tap dance to the tune of *Suwanee River*. I had rehearsed the scene dozens of times before, but my character's exit couldn't come quick enough, and I welcomed the dark of the backstage. I was unaware of any applause; I was too busy bent over the back stair railing trying to catch my breath.

Overall, the musical was a success, and as we made our final bow, members of the audience made their way to the foyer, waiting for the chance to congratulate each of the performers in person. A line was formed at the door, and soon I was shaking the hands of random people, smiling and thanking anyone who offered anything close to a compliment. The bottleneck in the narrow hall was making me claustrophobic. I kept my eye on the crowd, though, trying to figure out if Brian had dodged out the door early.

Without warning, a large hand clapped my back and my dad was pulling me into a squeezing hug. "You did such a good job! Who knew you had it in you? Your tap dance routine was hilarious!"

I tried to respond, but the air would not come. It was only when he released me that I was able to take a deep breath. "Thanks, Dad," I panted, readjusting my costume's top. He stepped to the side and I could see that mom was behind him with a rather ambiguous smile on her face. I had seen the look on her face many times before; she was holding back her criticisms with a front of politeness. "Did you like Bye Bye Birdie, Mom?"

Her lips pulled back tight so her closed mouth looked like a thin, straight line. "It was a high school production, after all, so..." She wandered off, not finishing her sentence purposely. A veritable insert-your-own-insult-here. She looked me up and down, taking in my cropped shirt and the tassels hanging from the bottom of the capris. "Your role was interesting," She commented, eyes focused on my midriff. I instinctively covered myself up. "We won't have to worry about you attracting boys anytime soon, if what we saw was any indication." She nudged Dad, hoping he would nod in agreement. He didn't. She sniffed. "That and the fact that she inherited *your* unremarkable features."

Somehow, despite this not being the first crooked comment she had thrown at me, I couldn't help but blink with wide eyes for several seconds in shock of it. Even my dad threw a warning look in her direction. I knew that my mom never really warmed up to the idea of me being in the musical, no matter how I tried proving that it didn't make an effect on my studies. "I guess if I don't have a boyfriend, that means I won't have any problems keeping my grades up, right?" My arms still cradled my concealed stomach.

She gave me a pointed look. "After all this distraction, I certainly hope so."

"Well, honey, let's give Alyssa a chance to greet some more people before she has to take off to the after-party." Dad came forward and hugged me again, gentler this time. "We really are proud of you, sweetie," he said as he backed up. "And we'll see you before midnight, remember."

I nodded, feeling a small stab of guilt at the fact that later that night I would not be where they thought I was. I covered it up by waving at Patrice, who was jerking her head in the direction of the changing rooms. "Yes! I'll be home in time, I promise." I started running back into the auditorium, heading backstage.

* * *

I CHANGED OUT OF MY revealing costume and worked as fast as I could at washing off the caked-on stage makeup. Brushing my hair back into a short ponytail, I was feeling much more myself. Compared to the stuffiness of the changing rooms, the chill of March sweeping around the parking lot was glorious. Most of the cars had already cleared out by then, with my mom's borrowed sedan being one of the last ones.

There, in the back of the parking lot, was an all-too-familiar truck. My heart leapt at the sight of it, and I hurried to unlock my passenger door so I could throw my bag on the seat. Checking to make sure that there was no one loitering, I adopted an unhurried pace and crossed the blacktop to the pickup. The windows were tinted, a tell-tale sign that this particular vehicle was from a sunnier state. It wasn't normal to see them up here in Washington, but at that moment I was grateful. It made a meeting like this less obvious. As I approached, the window was rolled down and Brian's face appeared. "So..." He said casually. "*Were* you stalking my truck?"

I thought back to that day, and my face reddened at the memory. "Yes. Yes I was." I affirmed.

"I thought so."

I went around the nose of the truck and let myself in, sliding into the passenger seat. With the click of the door, I let out a breath I hadn't known I was holding. "Wow." Brian only looked confused, so I explained myself. "It's just that... It's nighttime, and I'm in your truck. It all feels a little scandalous."

"Well, it *is* scandalous, to tell the truth." He leaned over and kissed me.

When he pulled back, I noticed that he was wearing jeans with a t-shirt and an open jacket. Not remembering if I had ever seen him in anything but his slacks and button-up shirts, I now appreciated this more casual look. "You're looking quite handsome in those jeans," I commented.

He looked down on himself before looking back up to me, briefly throwing his face in shadow. His eyes glittered. "You were looking pretty fetching in those heels. Shame you had to take off the blonde wig, though." I crossed the gap and aimed to playfully punch him on the arm, but he caught me and held me close to him. "Seriously, you did an amazing job, sweetheart."

It pleased me to hear him call me sweetheart, and I

hummed in contentment. "I'm glad you think so. Now I only have to repeat it three more times."

He lessened his grip on me, but didn't let me go. "Listen, ah..." Whatever he was about to say discomforted him, and he shifted a bit in his seat. This small movement caused my low self-esteem to kick in, and immediately doubts started to creep in and crawl about in my brain. I didn't have much time to put words to my thoughts before he explained himself. "I saw you with your parents in the foyer. I overheard your conversation."

I looked down at the floor, feeling a little exposed with his uncensored view of my relationship with them. "You did?"

"Let's just say that it helped explain some things about you."

I sat back. "Like?"

He sensed my unease and patted my hands to calm me. "Well, for one thing, I understand now why you strive so hard to be the top in my class, and in every other class, from what I've heard in the teacher's break room."

I shook my head. "I'm a perfectionist, I..."

He interrupted me. "No, I don't think you are. I think your *mother* is."

"She pushes me, it's true..."

"Too hard, by the look I saw on your face."

I started to protest, but his truth was like a needle that burst me open and I felt myself deflating in front of him. I sunk into the cushion. "All my life, I've been told over and over again that I am smart. *Only* smart. I never heard any other compliment pass her lips. I guess..." I searched for the right words. "I guess at some point I figured that it's all I've got going for me. So it's what I focus on. It's what gives me *meaning*." My river of confessions embarrassed me, and I hid my face in my hands to hide my immaturity.

But his gentle hands pried mine away and he cupped my chin, holding me there so when he leaned in close, my eyes were fixed on his. I could see them shining in the obscurity. "You don't have to hide from me," he murmured. I took a sharp intake of breath, trying to stave off tears, only to have one escape and trickle down to land on his upturned palm. "Alyssa, I never thought to ask you. And I'm sorry, I should have asked: Is this your first...?"

I couldn't control how my voice came out. "Relationship?" I squeaked.

"Is it?"

A blush flooded my cheeks. "Yes?"

"So you've had no one to love you just as you are and tell you all the things that make you wonderful?"

I shook my head furiously.

Brian's voice lowered, taking on the authoritative tone that I had heard him use countless times before when he was chiding errant students. "Then listen, Alyssa." Everything within me stilled, obeying the command. "Yes, you are smart." He looked into me, as if he was addressing my soul as he said this, and I could see his control over his own emotions failing. "But you are also beautiful, and funny, and kind, and so full of life! And it's a *damn* shame no one told you these things before." He kissed me, and I could taste the salt from my own lips. "You better learn to take compliments," he said softly, his warm breath brushing my cheek. "Because I don't know anyone else who deserves to hear them more than you."

I smiled timidly, simply amazed at his faith in me. "I don't know how I deserve *you*."

He chuckled. "The feeling's mutual, Julietta."

"I love you."

He bumped noses with me. "And I love you." A second passed, and a sigh. "Okay, enough with all this mushy sentimentalidad." He pressed into me, capturing my mouth and holding me steady with firm hands at the nape of my neck.

I felt myself surrender at the sensation, and with every kiss, I felt my insecurities lessen and lessen until the only thing left was bliss.

* * *

THE SOUND OF THE DOOR opening to the Physics classroom barely registered with me as I sat buried in my textbook, trying to look up the second law of thermodynamics. It was the study period at the end of our hour and a half, and conversation was kept to a minimum, therefore it was easy to hear the quick exchange between the main office page and the Physics teacher.

"Alyssa?" Hearing my name surprised me, and I looked up to see Mrs. Swartz standing near her desk with the page holding a rather large vase containing what looked like two dozen white roses. "These came for you."

Hushed *oohs* and *aaws* sounded out from amongst the female students, and I flushed sheepishly as I made my way to the front of the classroom to receive the gift. The page gratefully handed it off to me, and I could see why he was glad to be rid of it; the bouquet along with its leaded crystal holder had to weigh at least twenty pounds. I lugged it back to my desk and set it on the tabletop, not quite sure what to do with the flowered jungle now taking over my schoolwork.

"You are so lucky!" Hayley leaned over the aisle way toward me, her pencil falling on the floor with a clatter as she tried to get a better look at the blooms. "What does the card say? Who is it from?"

I looked where she was pointing, and there, nestled in between the rose buds, was a small white envelope that almost blended in with its surroundings. I opened it up and read the card inside. The text was printed, but there was no mistaking the voice behind the words:

Congratulations on your success on opening night. You were absolutely fantastic.

It's said that white roses represent new beginnings, so let this be a celebration of the beginning of 'us,' and of a life where you realize how amazing you truly are.

With much love,

B

I tried to control the emotions on my face, but I had to look down to hide the tears that were threatening to spill over my eyelashes. I couldn't hide the grin, though, and Hayley's interest was piqued to the point where she started bouncing in her seat. "Who's it from? Who's it from?"

I kept a straight face, tucking the card into my backpack before she had a chance to snag it from my hands. "My parents. They didn't bring me any flowers on opening night. Apparently they wanted to surprise me."

Upon hearing my lie, Hayley's expression went flat

in confusion. "Oh." She sounded disappointed. For a few moments it looked like she was going to challenge my answer, but eventually her mouth snapped shut and she turned back to her work.

After Physics, I carried the bouquet over to my locker in order to stash it away for the rest of the day. However, much to my chagrin, the arrangement was much too large and my skinny locker was much too small to fit the flowers in without crushing the delicate blossoms. I had a feeling that this was something that Brian was planning on, because for the rest of the day, I had to carry his gift from class to class, drawing curious looks from fellow students. At first I was embarrassed, but by the time I reached the final period and Spanish, I was starting to enjoy the attention that I was drawing.

Brian must have seen me coming with my arms full, because he held the door open for me so I could enter the classroom. "Looks like Julietta got some roses today." I shot him a look of faux annoyance, but his cool smile showed that he was clearly enjoying himself. I was setting the vase down on my desk in the front row just as Katalina strode in with Sancho and Pedro. Eyeing the flowers, she made a face that could only be interpreted as pure jealousy.

Pedro's eyebrows knit together. "Since when does Alyssa get flowers?" His tone was dripping with ridicule.

I could feel Brian's unspoken response floating in the air, his desire to insult Pedro practically tangible. In the corner of my eye, I saw him set his mouth in forced silence, but a nearly imperceptible nod was all I needed to spur me on. With him nearby, I felt brave enough to speak up for myself. I turned to face my fellow students, a smile of confidence upon my lips. "Apparently, *Pedro*, since now."

Inexplicably, Pedro ended up paired with me again for debates that afternoon.

dieciséis

APRIL COULDN'T SEEM TO MAKE up its mind, and I shrugged off my windbreaker and tied it around my waist. The weather was always changeable around this time of year, and I had learned over the years to layer up my tops so each one could be peeled off or thrown back on depending on what temperature it was at any given hour. At this moment, I was walking uphill with a backpack, two blocks away from my house, and already I was starting to break into a sweat.

I had told my parents that I was heading over to Hayley's house for that afternoon and evening for a Physics study session. I'm surprised that they didn't find that explanation suspicious with it being Hayley and a *Saturday*.

My dad was pulling on his worn, mud-covered sneakers in preparation to visit a client's future home site. "Do you need me to give you a ride over there, 'Lys?"

I took my hand off the doorknob and spun back to face my dad who was already reaching for his keys. "No, that's fine. It's warm enough out and I need to get some exercise, anyway. I've noticed recently that I'm sitting for practically, what, 50 plus hours a week as it is? Classes, homework... I'm going to start getting blood clots, Dad!"

It seemed over the top to my own ears, but my dad just shrugged and left the keys alone on their hook. "Just call if you need a ride back tonight."

"Hayley's got it covered. Bye, Dad!"

Now that my jacket was around my waist and I had reached the top of the hill, I had slowed my pace considerably, taking the time instead to appreciate the smells of new life in the air. Budding lilacs, fresh-cut grass, all mixed up with an all-pervading petrichor.

I hung a left and headed east, away from our downtown and further into the sleepy neighborhoods. I had specifically chosen a route that would lead me down roads seldom used by through traffic, but even so, I kept my eye out. The sunshine was drawing out the spring cleaners; old men with aerators and fertilizer were already prepping their lawns for summertime. One such senior saw me and waved. I didn't know him, but he probably had seen me before at a city function and recognized me as the councilwoman's daughter. I nodded back and lengthened my stride, hasty to pass his house. This town was too small and too proper, and gossip was a highly consumed commodity. If anyone even *suspected*... I shook my head at the uncomfortable thought and pressed on, coming to the end of the block and crossing the street.

I was at the point where I was getting chilly again and considering untying the windbreaker when the tan truck pulled up to my left and the passenger door opened with a click. Brian was leaning over the seat, arm outstretched as he pushed the door open wider. "Why hello there, beautiful!" He greeted with a smile.

I crinkled my nose at him and hopped off the sidewalk, slinging my backpack onto the floor of the passenger side and sliding in beside him. "Hola, amor," I purred, kissing him as the door shut behind me.

A hum of contentment filled his throat, and his fingers lingered for a second on the sensitive part of my neck before he drew himself back up and focused on pulling back onto the road. One hand expertly steered the wheel and the other remained next to me, which I took advantage of, slipping my fingers in between his and squeezing tightly. His thumb drew lazy circles into my palm. "It's simply *fantastic* that I'm seeing you on a Saturday," he commented, then added, "It feels downright normal, somehow."

I mused on that, letting my eyes wander off somewhere on the landscape passing us by. "If we were in different circumstances, I suppose." The words didn't seem right to me. "But not even then, not *really*." Before I had a chance to consider whether or not I should further voice my concern, the words came tumbling out of me. "When do we *ever* become normal?" I asked, turning back to look at his profile. "How do we even begin to explain us?"

It was a question that had obviously been bothering him as well. He set his jaw and reinforced his grip on my hand. "We don't," he answered simply.

The mood in the truck cab seemed to darken considerably, and I could feel my stomach start to churn at the silence that ensued. I couldn't help though the train of thinking that started to barrel through my mind. "So, how far is your house from here?" I could see the beginnings of pastures as we passed out of Lynn Creek.

"We're only about 20 minutes out. I live on the far side of Dukwibal Bay."

"Because I was thinking... I've never been to your house before, and we're going to be *extremely* alone..."

I could tell that he was waiting for me to finish my unspoken question by the curious tilt of his head, and I fidgeted, feeling uncomfortable with what I was about to say.

He noticed me shifting in my seat. "Yes?"

Caution was thrown to the wind, but I felt it needed to be said. "I know we've been together for over a month now, and I *do* love you, but I'm not sure I'm ready to..."

Brian visibly started, and his eyes were suddenly off the road and piercing mine. "Is *that* what you're worried about?!" The sheer surprise in his voice made me feel idiotic for asking, so I didn't reply. He cursed in Spanish and went on anyway. "Of course, not! You don't even have to worry about that, do you understand?"

I nodded, still not saying anything.

Visibly upset, he took a deep breath to calm down. "In the first place, Alyssa, I want you to know that I love you. And *because* I love you, I respect you and would never want to put you in *any* compromising position." The stress in his words left little room for me to doubt him. "Secondly: not if, but *when* we become 'normal,' I want to be above reproach in all of this. I want to do this in a right and proper fashion."

"As much as *can* be proper in the given circumstances," I amended.

"In the given circumstances," he agreed.

We reached the coastline, and I spent some time staring out the passenger side window and appreciating the sun glinting off the rough ocean waves. Somehow the view was appropriate and comparable to what I was currently feeling. Stresses and doubts came to try my steadfastness, but Brian's love was warm and reassuring, making everything beautiful. I had said it already, but... "I love you, Brian."

He lifted the hand that was still clasped in his and kissed it lightly, and even though I wasn't looking in his direction, I knew he was smiling. I could feel his lips against my knuckles.

It turns out that his house was small, white, and very compact. Thanks to my dad's penchant for discussing work at the dinner table, I was easily able to identify it as an early 1900s house. Its boxy design was popular in the port towns of this coast since the construction was quick and fairly simple. This made for a cozy, yet cramped living room with doors on nearly every wall leading to the adjacent rooms. The hallways were non-existent.

After hanging up my jacket in the small entry area, Brian invited me to poke my nose around the rooms; he must have seen my face light up in curiosity. There were two bedrooms, one that was currently being used as an office and catch-all. Beside a well-used desk with stacks of papers, there was a bookshelf *overloaded* with books. Spanish titles and old school annuals were calling my name, but there were other rooms to be seen. I left my perusal of them for later.

When it came to looking in at where he slept, a weird feeling settled in the pit of my stomach.

I decided to skip over that room and inspect the kitchen instead.

After noting the bike parked on the back stoop through the window and taking a peek at the simple dining table that was loaded with laundry and books and clearly not used as an actual place to eat, I came back into the living room, where Brian was waiting for me. He was sitting on a paisley couch that reminded me of something I had seen once at my grandmother's house. Heck, he probably *did* buy it off of some grandmother's yard sale. I sat down next to him, noting the blank walls. "So, not much of a decorator, are we?"

He laughed, knowing that I was only poking fun. "No. I don't really have much of a sense for that." He flushed a bit, looking a bit embarrassed. "I didn't have much time for cleaning, so you'll have to excuse the mess."

"It's fine. Really. My room is just as ridiculous."

His good-humored *harrumph* indicated that he caught my underhanded poke at the state of his bachelor pad, and scooted over closer to me. "Well, I suppose we had probably get started on our work, but first, I just need to get this out of the way..." He wrapped his arms around me and pressed a lingering kiss on my jawline. I shivered under the touch and I turned so I could properly face him.

His dark eyes were intense and filled with a passion that made heat build up inside me like the steady onset of a summer sunrise. "I'm glad you're here," he said, leaning in to capture my lips in a searing kiss, and I allowed myself to melt in his embrace, sighing into his mouth.

But just as soon as it came, it was gone, and he nimbly leapt up from the couch and in the direction of his office, looking particularly gleeful at the sight of me put out. "I hope you're prepared to study for at least a couple of hours." He came back into view, a trio of large folders in hand. "I have lower level midterms to grade." I looked at the amount of paperwork in his hands with wide eyes, and he laughed. "What? Did you think that my workweek ended when the bell rang?"

I shook my head and picked up my backpack out of the entry and fished out my Physics textbook and my notebook, opening to my notes for the last session and setting it on the coffee table. "I've got some flash cards to make, and then I was just going to recheck my answers on my Trig assignment," I told him.

As I was searching for my pencils, Brian looked over my shoulder at my Physics notes. "Alyssa Kessler!" He said in a slightly accusatory tone. "Are you a... *doodler*?"

I looked back down at my notes, at the Roman columns, flowers, and vines scrawled all over my pages. "...Um?" was all I could say.

"You *never* doodle in my class. *Nunca*."

I rolled my eyes. "Well, of *course* not in your class, Señor. I'm too easily absorbed in whatever you have to say to even think about it." *It doesn't help that you're amazing to look at,* I noted to myself. "But when I'm in a class where some other student is making the teacher explain the same concept for the third time in a row, I have to find ways to pass the time." I took my pencil and added a leaf to one of the vines.

"Well, I can't say I blame you," he remarked, and tousled my hair as he made his way to a side chair, letting me have free reign of the sofa area.

Our attentions were taken up by our respective assignments and over the course of the next couple hours we worked in companionable silence. I would sneak a peek over at him occasionally, appreciating the grace with which he corrected papers, some of which seemed to be murdered with red pen. He would catch me watching him out of his peripheral and smirk in acknowledgment, which would send my eyes flying back to the task at hand.

I had moved from the coffee table to the floor, my notes spread out in piles according to chapter, and each were accompanied by flash cards that were highlighted in various colors. Keywords and concepts were in blue, and the scientists and their discoveries were being highlighted in gree...

A chuckle forced me to look back up again, and Brian must have completed his grading some time ago, because he looked settled in as he watched me from across the room. "Find something funny?" I asked lightly.

"You look like a bird in a kaleidoscope nest." He laughed.

Sticking my tongue out at him playfully, I started recompiling my papers and placing them back in their respective places in my binder.

Brian stood up and stretched, a loud *pop* emanating from his shoulder. "Feeling like you might be ready for dinner?" His question was accompanied by him tucking away folders into his over-the-shoulder bag.

I looked up from my backpack. "I think so, yeah. Do you want me to help you?"

"Now it would be rude if I asked a guest of mine to lend a hand," Brian replied cheerily. He made his way to the kitchen, continuing as he went. "Feel free to make yourself at home. I know you're *dying* to sift through my bookshelves."

He knew me only too well. "Don't mind if I do," I replied, watching as he rummaged through one of his cupboards, appreciating the tone in his arms as he reached over his head to grab down dishes.

"You're staring at me again," he teased, not taking

his eyes off his task.

"Can't a girl just enjoy the view?"

"¡Vete!"

"Okay, I'm going, I'm going."

Upon further inspection of the bookcase, I found there were multiple volumes with which I could entertain myself for hours: yearbooks from several different high schools and a couple from his years in college, the copy of *Steams Are Less Than Rivers* that we had discussed once upon an afternoon, and binders full of past lesson plans and notes. There was no rhyme or reason to his method of shelving, and my fingers itched to pull things out and create some order out of chaos. One small paperback caught my eye, and I pulled it out to take a better look and found it was an English-to-Spanish dictionary that had clearly seen better days. Part of the orange cover was missing and some of the binding had come undone. Opening to the first page, I saw something written in a messy script: *Property of Brian Brown – No toca!*

I shouted over to him. "So this must have belonged to you *before* you realized that you conjugated 'tocar' wrong."

He leaned around the door frame of the kitchen, showing how tiny the house was by taking three strides to the study, and looked at what I was holding. "That's what

I thought you were looking at. It's my first Spanish dictionary."

"Did you buy it for the missions trip you took in middle school?"

"You remember that? Wait, of course you do. What was I thinking?" His ramble followed him back to his dinner preparations.

Placing the dictionary back on the shelf, it occurred to me that I hadn't yet seen any pictures of Brian and his life before Washington. Several unlabeled photo albums were bundled together on a lower shelf, and, not sure what I was looking for, I grabbed a leather-bound one from the middle and settled myself back on the living room couch so I could take my time.

Faces that I didn't know greeted me. Though I could tell that this was a celebration of some sort, I had no way of putting the photos into any meaningful context. The date on the developed exposures indicated that what I was looking at only occurred three years ago. After a couple of pages of smiling people holding glasses of champagne, Brian finally showed up, looking very handsome in formal slacks and a dark purple dress shirt with matching tie. He was with an older woman who was unmistakably his mother, from whom he clearly inherited his warm, brown eyes. A brunette woman had situated herself in the gap between them, pulling a silly face for the camera. This was most likely Michelle. Brian was right; I liked her already.

The party had been held at a banquet hall that was open to views of the ocean, and pictures of Brian and another woman leaning against the patio railing were set in the foreground of a sunset. She had to be only a few inches shorter than Brian, with cropped hair that I could tell was naturally blonde and a face with distinct, delicate features. Her stunning looks were matched by a glamorous, pale pink cocktail dress and a smile that radiated off the page. It didn't take me long to realize that she was attending this event alongside him. Several of the pictures had the two in close proximity, Brian's arm wrapped protectively around her waist. A knot started to form in my stomach, and with my suspicions roused, I flipped a couple pages forward. A photo showed the crowd raising their glasses and toasting, cheering on as Brian and the beautiful blonde woman were wrapped up in a fierce kiss.

This was an engagement party.

This was *Brian's engagement party.*

I instantly felt stupid when faced with this reality. How could it have not occurred to me that Brian may have very well been married before? What was I even doing? The lack of any relationship experience on my part and the immaturity of my ways bore down on me. When I compared my haphazard existence to the poise and elegance of the woman in these pictures, I felt nothing but small. The gap that I had told myself didn't exist between us opened up once more.

Another second and I would have sunken into the old, wooden floor had Brian's voice not served as a life preserver. "Are you okay, Alyssa?"

Blinking out of my unfocus, my eyes made contact with Brian, who was setting a plate of spaghetti in front of me on the coffee table. "How do you put up with me, really?" I asked. "I'm childish, impulsive, not to mention emotional..." My voice was evenly toned as I willed myself to be calm.

Concern flooded Brian's face. "What brought this on?" He looked down to see the open photo album on my lap and the corner of his mouth twitched. "Aah." He took a seat next to me, and despite the awkwardness of the topic, he didn't leave any room between us, his thigh flush with mine. "Do you want me to explain what this is?" He indicated the photos.

"Does it ever bother you that I'm only eighteen, Brian?"

"Can I put that question aside for now and tell you a story first?"

Huffing, angry with myself for even making this a big deal, I closed the album. I could tell that Brian wasn't trying to avoid answering me. Nothing in his body language spoke of agitation, only patience. So I closed my eyes for a second to center myself and nodded, waiting for him to begin.

"So, about five years back, I met Samantha through a mutual friend. She was sweet, outgoing... a *nice* girl. We had a lot in common and everything seemed to be clicking, and everyone loved her, my friends, my family. My mom couldn't stop talking about her. And then Michelle goes and gets married to Robert, and ideas start turning around in my head. I'm not getting any younger, and Samantha and I got along really well, so marriage was the next logical step. I felt it was what I was *supposed* to do. You know, the right thing?" He paused, and when I opened my eyes, he was checking my face to see if I was tracking with him. I nodded again to reassure him.

He continued. "In addition to this, there was so much prodding from every side and before I knew it, I was proposing and plans were being made and dates set... I suppose I was happy, and everything was going as planned, and then..." Brian's hands spread out to signify everything going up in smoke. "She broke it off. She left. At first I didn't understand why, but when she said she didn't want me to marry her because I felt *obligated* to, well..." He reached over to take my hand. "I suppose in some ways I took a teaching job up here to get a fresh start. I needed to clear my head. And then I met Amy and I realized I was starting the whole bad cycle again."

He let the words fall between us, giving me time to soak in everything he had just shared with me. A question bubbled out of me before I had time to edit. "So where do I fit in with all of this?"

"You see, that's the thing!" Suddenly his voice brightened. He shifted so he was fully facing me now. "Whether or not this is something I'm *supposed* to be doing, all I know is that I can't *stand* not having you in my life. I *want* this. I want *you*."

My eyes prickled and I knew tears weren't far off. "But doesn't it bother you?" I asked, bringing back the question that was left on the back burner, threatening to boil over. "That I'm young and immature? Everyday I'm afraid that you'll wake up and realize that you're wasting your time with... with a *girl*..." I felt the warm droplets tracking down my cheeks already. Why was I always crying in front of him?

He picked up my hand and held it safely between both of his. "It does bother me, yes, and it's because I'm afraid, too." His dark eyes were stormy, anxious. "I'm afraid that someday you'll outgrow me and I won't be what you want anymore."

And there we were. Both vulnerable. Both wanting to prove the other wrong. I threw the album to the floor and closed the gap between us, my arms around his neck, my forehead touching his. "That will never happen," I said fervently, a spell to ward off any other wayward truth. It was sealed with a kiss that only made me hungry for more.

Brian recovered first. "By the way, your food is getting cold."

I rolled my eyes.

* * *

"YOU CAN STOP HERE." I instructed. Brian pulled over to the curb, the driveway to my house in sight only a block away, and turned off the engine. With the headlights switched off, I could only see him by the glow of the stereo. The CD that I had burned him back in November was softly playing in the background, and it provided an interesting soundtrack to the swaying trees and rustling leaves. I pretended to be absorbed in what was going on outside my window, my fingernails scratching against the stiff cloth of my seatbelt.

"It's only going to get harder, you know," Brian said, and I turned back to him.

"The whole having to leave you thing? Spending my nights counting down the time when I get to see you again?"

He only sighed in response. Clearly I was not alone in this.

I unbuckled myself and sunk into his side. "I hate this. I really do."

He freed his arm and wrapped it around my shoulders, pressing a kiss to my forehead. "Todo estará bien, mi amor." (Everything will be alright, my love.) His words, whispered into my hair, should have provided me comfort, but I let out a whimper of doubt. He tightened his grip on me. "Someday, not long from now, we'll run away together, just like Manuel and Isabel."

I frowned at the comparison. "You know as well as I do that they didn't meet a good end."

"True, but your father isn't a wealthy, Uruguayan aristocrat, as far as I know."

"You are correct."

"See? Then we're golden." He unbuckled his own seat belt and ducked down so I could see his face, see the sincerity in his eyes. "I believe we're worth waiting for. Do you?"

I nodded, breathless.

My face was taken into his hands and a kiss, lingering, warm, and full of longing, was pressed to my lips. "We will *have* a 'normal,' do you hear me?" Brian's voice was low, fevered.

I had to close my eyes at the threat of disorientation.

"Do you promise?"

"I promise."

And before I could find myself doing something rash, I grabbed my bag and removed myself from temptation, slipping out the passenger door. I put my hand on the glass barrier that was now between us, the interior of the cab now obscured from my view. A couple more deep breaths, crystallized and swirling around me, and I was on my way back to my own front door.

My head told me that we were still not free, that there was no way to know what was coming for us. My heart, however, was flooded with hope, and hope was beyond rationality.

Neither of us slept that night.

diecisiete

"¿ESTÁN LISTOS PARA EL EXAMEN, clase? Tenemos sola una semana más!" (Are you ready for the exam, class? We only have one more week!)

Señor Brown received a response without delay.

"¡*No*!" We cried in unison. Sancho further illustrated our point by falling out of his chair and playing dead on the industrial carpet.

Brian laughed good-naturedly. "No hay tiempo para preocuparnos. Tenemos mucho trabajo antes el gran día." (There isn't time to get worried. We have too much work before the big day.) Starting with me at the front, he dropped discs on each of our desks, labeled with his slanted handwriting. "Para practicar sus habilidades de comprender y responder, he creido este disco. Necesitan escuchar a mi voz increíble y responder a mis preguntas por escrito. Esbriban dos párrafos de cuatro lineas por cada pregunta, por lo menos." (To practice your comprehension and response skills, I have created this disc. You all need to listen to my incredible voice and respond to my questions with writing. Write two paragraphs of at least four sentences for every question.)

Yolanda raised her hand. "¿Cuántas preguntas hay en el disco?" (How many questions are there on the disc?)

"Diez." (Ten)

I groaned along with my fellow students, but we were drowned out by the school bell.

"Due on Monday!" Brian shouted out into the cacophony of zipping backpacks and mutters of anxiety. I watched with amusement the irritation in his face from being ignored before tending to my papers and putting things away.

The penultimate student closed the door behind him noisily and I turned back to grin at my flustered boyfriend. "You are absolutely *insane*, you know that?"

His attention was instantly on me. "Hey, you knew what you were signing up for." He squinted at me for greater effect.

I took his ribbing with good stride. "Well, I don't

know..." I rubbed my chin thoughtfully.

Brian leaned far over his podium, hovering inches from my face. "You look lovely today, by the way." The compliment was followed by a kiss to my temple.

I blushed, glad that he noticed and appreciated the effort I had made that morning. My hands smoothed out the folds in my floral-printed sundress. "Didn't know I was signing up for *this*, for one." I said, flashing him a coquettish purse of my lips.

He smiled and crossed over to seat himself at the desk next to me, sinking down and flopping his head back as though exhausted. "God, this day. We're on the countdown for the AP exam, and I starting to get a little worried about you guys."

"I'll be fine. I think. If you don't kill me with homework first."

"I'm seriously impressed, 'Lys. Despite the distraction of 'us,' you're staying on task. *We're* staying on task." His eyes shifted so he was making eye contact with me and no longer looking at the ceiling. "Speaking of, during the study session, you were most definitely humming 'Cada Día' when you were working on your multiple choice."

I rested my chin on the heel of my hand. "*Cada día, yo quiero morir...*" I crooned, enjoying Brian's smirk and the twinkle in his eye. *"Porque tu estás enfrente de mí, y no puedo tocarte..."*

"You know," He said, "I would have never loaned you that CD if I knew you were going to do nothing but torture me with it."

I rolled my eyes. "What can I say? I just can't help myself." I slipped out of my seat and joined him, perching myself on one of Brian's knees. My arms found their way around his neck and the full length of my torso was pressed into him. Only a couple inches of space was left between our lips, and I thoroughly enjoyed the frustration that I was causing him by refusing to close the gap. As I sat there contemplating the curve of his jawline, something occurred to me. "Brian?"

"Mmm?"

By his lazy, complacent reply, it was clear that I could have asked him to do just about anything in that moment. I pushed away the wayward thoughts that started to form in my mind and refocused myself. "I've got some good news."

"What's that?"

I let a pause linger before answering. "I was accepted into Berkeley."

The sudden jolt that came from Brian sitting up nearly caused me to fall off my perch and I held onto his neck for dear life. "You did?! When did this happen?"

"The acceptance packet arrived on Monday."

"It's Friday." It was a statement, but I caught the unspoken question.

I shrugged. "I suppose I was just a tad nervous."

The little wrinkle that formed in between his eyebrows was endearing. "Nervous about telling me?"

The way he said it made me feel the slightest bit guilty. "It's just that the last time I mentioned college..." *You acted uncomfortable*, I thought, but I changed course and started again. "I just needed time to process, that's all. I mean, Berkeley!"

"That's amazing, sweetheart. It really is." Brian caught me up in his arms and buried his face in my neck, and I flushed with the sensation, but I had noticed his smile waver before his face dipped from my view. When he surfaced, it was to change the subject. "So, can I pick you up on Saturday?"

I laughed at his eagerness, pushing myself back to my feet and busying myself with my backpack. "Tomorrow should be fine, but we've got to slow it down a bit. Hayley *never* studies that often, and the fact that we've been meeting for the last three weeks? It's bound to look suspicious. Or I could just tell my parents that I'm heading over to my teacher's house to snog him senseless.

They would find it so ludicrous that they would automatically believe the alternative."

Brian laughed along with me, finding the humor in our ridiculous situation. "To be on the safe side, I'm going to say 'no' to that."

* * *

DESPITE OUR BETTER JUDGMENT, WE both agreed, however, that once more couldn't hurt.

"What's this?" I asked while I was divesting my jacket in Brian's entry. The living room had been rearranged, sofa and coffee table pushed to the back to block his bedroom door. The exposed floor was covered with a quilt and what looked like every pillow he owned. A blue screen on his small television glowed, indicating that he had something queued up for this evening.

"Well," he said, the excitement palpable in the bounce of his movements as he rushed about the room. "I was thinking we could watch a movie tonight, and oops, pardon the mess..." He grabbed the laundry basket I had side-stepped and with two steps vaulted over the couch and ducked into the bedroom. He emerged again with one more pillow that he tossed onto the pile. "It just seemed that this would be more, um..." He scratched the back of his neck, seeming a bit shy all of a sudden.

"Romantic?" I supplied, amused a bit at his flushed

face. "I agree," and I slipped off my shoes and sat on the floor, choosing a couple choice pillows and propping myself up with them. I patted the floor beside me and Brian obediently sunk down cross legged a few inches away. Feeling brazen, I pushed myself forward, my hands finding their purchase on both of his knees, leaning into and invading his space. "Did you miss me?" I asked.

A groan emanated from his throat. "Maybe this was a bad idea." Brian's voice was impossibly low.

I could sense the heat rolling off him, the desire burning behind his dark look and it felt exhilarating to wield that kind of power. Recklessness took over my better judgment, and I tilted my head closer, the tip of my nose nearly touching his. "A bad idea?" I shifted my hands back slightly, fingernails scraping denim. "Well in that case..."

"Just come here," he rumbled, snaking his hands into my hair and pulling me to him by the nape of my neck. I smiled and gave into his kiss, matching his frenzy, losing track of whose heartbeat was whose.

It barely took a tug and I took him backward with me, his weight pressing down on me in a way that felt delicious. His lips left mine, hot kisses trailing to my collarbone. *Sweet heaven...*

My gasp of surprise must have broken the spell, because he stiffened at the noise. "Damnit," came his muffled groan of frustration. He rolled over on his back, head still touching mine, and we both caught our breath, staring up at his eggshell ceiling. "We can't be doing this, 'Lys." He was slowly regaining his composure.

I propped my head up on my elbow, looking down at him amused. "I don't know what you mean, Brian?" I reached over, tracing his jawline.

He snatched my hand up, capturing it and holding it. "The hell you don't," he growled playfully. He kissed my fingers before releasing me, and I lowered myself back, content to lie there with him, side by side. "You gotta stop making it so hard for me." Brian's detached voice floated up into the air above us.

"But it's too much fun," I countered.

"Be that as it may, *Cariña*..."

"*Cariña*? Hmm..." It was something he had already called me multiple times before, *sweetheart*, but in that moment it struck me as something so casual, so *comfortable*, that it filled me with a warm turning deep inside. It wasn't the fluttering of passion and novelty, but of something that promised to expand, place roots, and ripen. I sought out his hand beside me and felt his fingers ready to interlace with mine. Together we contemplated the ceiling in companionable silence, tracing the cracks in the corners, the settling foundation.

After a few moments, Brian broke the silence.

"Jasmine." He said matter-of-factly.

"What?" I asked, turning my head to look at him once again.

His eyes were already on me. "Your perfume. It's jasmine. I noticed when I was, ah..." A brief, self-conscious pause. "When I was studying the curve of your lovely neck." One of his signature lop-sided grins made an appearance.

"Oh?"

"Is it new? I don't remember you wearing perfume before."

"It is. I saw it in the department store and it occurred to me that I actually have a boyfriend to wear perfume for now." His spare hand had started running through my hair, and I leaned into his touch. "What do you think?"

He considered the question, and answered with a story. "In the summers growing up, all of us kids in my neighborhood would spend the evenings organizing *huge* games of hide-and-seek. All down the street, up in the trees, in backyards where we didn't belong, where-ever. And I don't know who had it in their garden, but the cool air always smelled of night-blooming jasmine. It was everywhere." His eyes were focused on me, but his voice was wistful, far away. "It's funny how smells connect you to memories like that, but every time I smell jasmine anymore, it reminds me of being free, of being young and wild."

Brian's words painted a vivid picture for me, and for a second I could imagine that his memories were my own. I was running through a redolent night. "So you like it, then?"

"Yeah, it suits you." He stayed his hand, cradling me. "It's beautiful," he murmured softly. "You're beautiful."

I blushed. "Brian?"

"Yeah?"

I cleared my throat. "I, uh, I have a question about the fourth prompt on the CD..."

I was answered with a pillow to the face. "¡Basta! Can't help you, Julietta, you know that."

"But I'm not sure what tense you're expecting me to answer in?!"

"Argh! Señor Brown no está aquí." He reached for another pillow.

Giggling, I easily ducked his half-hearted throw, sitting up and leaning my weight against him. "Fine!" I huffed. "You said we have a movie to watch?"

* * *

I WOKE UP LATE ON Sunday morning, my first thoughts being that of the night before and what a glorious Saturday it had been. My good mood refused to be sullied even when I rolled over and took in the hurricane-like state of my room. Clearly Brian's organizational habits were starting to rub off on me. Throwing off my comforter, I settled my feet on the floor and prepared myself for a day of cleaning.

About an hour into decompiling stacks of papers and sorting laundry, Dapper scratched on my door to be let in. The distraction brought to my attention that it was almost noon and I had yet to even shower or eat anything. Time certainly flies when you are having fun. I pulled my hair back into a messy ponytail and was slipping on a bathrobe in order to remedy this when my cell rang. There could only be two people that would be calling me, and when I picked up, it was my favorite of the two. "If you're wondering if I have finished your ridiculously long assignment yet, the answer is no," I teased him.

"I just want you to be ready," Brian answered, chuckling. "The exam is *this* Wednesday, Julietta."

"Oh, so *now* Señor Brown makes an appearance? Are you calling all of us Advanced Placement students today as a courtesy, or am I just special?"

"You're most definitely special." He affirmed, then added more earnestly, "If our relationship has in any way been detrimental to your success on this exam, I will have failed as your teacher."

I made a humming noise in disapproval.

"I'm serious, Alyssa."

"I know you are," I replied, separating the whites from my collected dirty laundry. "And the assignment will absolutely be finished by this evening, I promise."

"Thank you."

"By the way, last evening was lovely." My spare hand curled around the over-long cuff of my robe, idly energetic in response to the memories that floated back to my mind's surface. We had watched the movie-adaptation of *De La Libertad y Amor Agridulce*.

"You liked the movie?" He asked eagerly.

"Among other things," I said, thinking back also to our close proximity in the dark and the kisses that accompanied it. A loneliness for him stirred within me even though I could hear him breathing on the other end of the line. It struck me dumb for a moment.

"Are you replaying the same thing I am?" Brian's voice was warm and rolling with desire.

"Yeah," I answered, feeling winded. "And in case you couldn't already guess, I'm thinking about how much I love you right now."

"Are you now?" Came the playful response.

About to answer in the affirmative, I was interrupted by a tone in my ear. A colorful curse left my lips, and I rushed to explain myself before Brian questioned me. "Someone's on the other line. I've got to go."

"Ah. It's just as well. I'm not helping you get your homework done by distracting you."

I laughed. "A welcome distraction."

"I love you." He reminded me.

I hummed happily, then added, "See you Monday." His *adios* came through the line and a couple seconds later I switched over. "Hey, Hayley."

There was no delay, no greeting on Hayley's part. "Where were you last night?"

I remained calm and tried to think up a clever lie, but coming up with none I switched to the defensive. "What are you, my mom?" I cringed at how childish it sounded.

Hayley snorted. "No, but your mom called me last night when you didn't answer your phone. She asked me when we were going to finish studying, and I covered for you. I'd like to think that I saved your ass for a good reason, so you owe me an explanation."

I wasn't prepared for this line of questioning. "Can we talk about it later? I've got a ton of homework to get done..."

She sidestepped my excuse easily. "I saw you get into a truck a couple weeks ago nearby my house. I just happened to be looking out the window. What have you been doing?"

My stomach flipped uncomfortably. "Well, it's nothing dangerous if that's what you're worried about. I'm not off dealing crack in the mean streets of Lynn Creek or something."

"That's not funny." Hayley said, sounding as serious as I've ever heard her.

I sat down on my bed blindly and ended up nearly squishing Dapper, who let out a howl and jumped down to seek solace in my closet. I took a page from my cat's book and chose to hide as well. "Hayley, I don't want to talk about it."

Hayley didn't accept that. "You *never* talk to me anymore. I hardly see you, and now you want me to lie to your parents?" Her words were like a knife dipped in liquid guilt, tearing through my stomach. "Alyssa, I'm your best friend. And I'm worried about you. Why can't you tell me?"

I held my tongue, trying to prevent my panic from expelling words that I would regret. I couldn't blame her for being worried. It wasn't like me to lie about my whereabouts, wasn't like me to be stupid and take rides with boys. But how would I even begin to explain myself to Hayley? Could I even trust her with my secret? But then, it wasn't just *my* secret to keep. I decided to settle with a half-truth, hoping the grain of honesty would satisfy her appetite. "My parents can't know, alright?"

I could practically hear her lean forward in anticipation. "Know what?"

"I... sort of... have a boyfriend."

The reaction was immediate. "I knew it! Who is he? Why can't your parents know?"

"You know my parents. Anything that takes my attention away from my studies..." The lie tumbled easily from my lips.

"But who is he? Is he a senior?"

I cut off her questions before we treaded down a dangerous path of stories that I would be unable to recount later. "Look, can we just drop it?" Hoping my voice was stern enough to convince her, I continued. "I'll tell you about it, but not right now. It's too complicated."

There was huffing and muttering on the other end, then finally a "Fine," followed by, "But you promise you'll tell me later?"

"Later." I affirmed, leaving out the *much, much later* that was intended. I picked at the tie on my robe, pulling off the loose threads that hung there. "So, you went on a date with Shawn on Friday?" If memory served me right, she had been babbling about something along those lines all during lunch that day.

The proffered bait was taken. "Yes! Oh my gosh!" Hayley's voice raised another octave. She then proceeded to launch into a long-winded account of every detail of their movie outing together, including what the junior boy was wearing and how it was *so cute* and *can you believe what he did when he walked me to my door*? Throughout her speech I was barely listening, taking advantage of her redirected attention to scrape together my own fractured thoughts.

dieciocho

"JULIETTA?"

I LINGERED NEAR THE doorway, taking the initiative and switching off the overhead lights once I had seen that he had all of his things packed up. "¿Sí, Señor?"

Everything was tinged blue from the cloud-filtered sunlight that weakly lit the now-silent classroom. Brian passed the window and threw himself into the shadow with me, laying claim to my hips with gentle hands and pulling me close to him. "I just want to wish you good luck tomorrow." He said, leaning in to kiss me in the delicate way that always made me feel precious, worshiped. "You'll be amazing, as you always are." His smile was brilliant even in the cobalt dim.

Humming happily, I reached up and smoothed out an errant lock of hair on the crown of his head, something that had been on my nerves for the past hour and only now did I have the opportunity to do something about. I cupped his cheek with my hand, his face clean-shaven and smooth as he leaned into my touch. "I'll certainly try to be," I asserted. "For you, I always try to be."

He mirrored my motions by reaching back and smoothing his hand over the side of my own hair, grabbing my ponytail and giving it a playful tug. "Yo te amará, no importan los resultados." (I will love you, no matter your results.)

"Even if I fail?"

He pulled a face. "Well, that changes things..." I pinched him through his shirt and he jerked out of my reach, laughing. "But seriously," Brian said, grabbing the offending hand and holding it steady. "Are you sure you're ready for tomorrow?"

"Yes, sir."

"And you're going to review all your notes and vocab tonight?"

"You know who you're talking to, right?"

"Right, right. And you have your ride to get to the school early?"

"Check. Hayley's giving me a lift. She has zero period for a lab make-up."

"And did I mention that I love you?"

"Check, check, and double-check." A kiss on the lips made for an end to his questions. My toes were extended as far as they could go so that I could reach his lofty height. "Don't worry, Brian. Everything will be fine. And after that we'll have smooth sailing."

My beau leaned his back against the wall and drew my body with him. "Speaking of sailing, once summer starts and we finally have a bit more freedom and time to ourselves, I would love for you to come kayaking with me. We could turn it into a trip, a celebration of sorts. A Thank-God-I-Am-Only-Your-Boyfriend-Now-And-No-Longer-Your-Teacher celebration."

"Mmm. Sounds nice."

"You, me, and the San Juan Islands."

"Count me in."

I was treated to one last kiss, a soft one in the corner of my closed eye. "I'll see you tomorrow."

"Okay."

"Sleep well, amor."

"Y a tí, tambien."

* * *

HAYLEY'S HATCHBACK SHUDDERED AS SHE eased on her brake. Apparently the pressure wasn't enough; the tires slammed into the concrete barrier of the parking space and we came to a sudden halt. The rest of the Lynn Creek High School lot was fairly vacant with it being an hour before the start of first period. I saw Sancho tumble out of his station-wagon, gripping a coffee in one hand and dragging his backpack with the other, wearing an empty expression on his face that showed he was running on very little sleep.

"God, I gotta get to the lab. Mrs. Swartz is only giving us an hour and I'm already 5 minutes late," rushed Hayley, grabbing her things from the back seat.

I followed suit and we both stepped out into the morning air. Everything smelled cold and fresh, and I took a deep breath to encourage wakefulness. Despite all my efforts, my nervousness prevented me from enjoying a restful night.

"Are you coming?" Hayley was already several feet ahead of me, anxious to get inside.

"Wait up!" I exclaimed and quickly caught up to her, matching her stride.

We crossed the senior parking lot diagonally and were cutting through the staff parking when Brian's truck pulled in, metallic tan paint shimmering briefly in the early sun. He parked in his usual space, about 20 feet ahead of where Hayley and I were walking. I endeavored to keep to my straight path, but Hayley stiffened behind me, temporarily stilled by the truck in front of her. Looking back at her, she shot me a quick glance before resuming her pace.

Brian was slamming his door as we passed, adjusting the book bag on his shoulder. I made eye contact with him and he gave me a genial smile. "Good morning," he greeted, acknowledging both of us.

"Morning, Señor." My response came through the curtain of my hair, my head bowed. Hayley had started to increase her speed, and I looked over my shoulder at him as I chased after her.

I was unable to catch her until we had entered the building and were walking down the freshman hallway, her gait now agitated. I intended to walk with her until our paths diverged past the entrance to the courtyard. "See you after..." I started to say, making my left turn toward the library where the exam would take place.

Instead she grabbed my arm.

As she started dragging me to the girl's bathroom, I could see her face in front of me, tight-lipped and furious. It wasn't until we were tucked into the tiled corner that she really looked at me, making me wince at her ferocity.

"What the *hell*, Alyssa?"

My panic forced me to play dumb, even though I knew it was a bad move. "I don't know what..."

Hayley shook her head, blonde hair flying, and I felt the need to back up against the wall to put some space between us. "*Stop lying*, Alyssa! You're absolute shit at it."

I didn't respond, feeling paralyzed.

"It was *his* truck! It was Mr. Brown's truck!" Her voice was filled with complete certainty, pitch raising higher with every syllable. "What the hell are you doing spending time alone with Mr. Brown? He's a *teacher*!"

"You wouldn't understand..." I started, feeling completely inept. Unable to finish my sentence, Hayley stepped in, taking advantage of my pause.

"What is it that I don't understand, huh? First I see you getting into Brown's truck, and then you tell me that you have a boyfriend?" She wiped at her face, probably a physical attempt to erase some unsavory thought. A hand was laid on my jacket sleeve, and she fisted the fabric in desperation. "Don't you get how *dangerous* this is? He's probably telling you a whole bunch of stuff just so he can get into your pants, if he hasn't already..."

My silence slowly melted away in the heat of my anger. It was one thing to accuse me of lying, but the unfairness of questioning Brian's intentions brought a sharpness to my focus, a target to lash out at. "Stop, Hayley."

"So he has, then?"

I glared at her. "Shut up, Hayley! You don't know what you're talking about. It's not like that. You don't know *anything* about Brian and me."

Hayley took a harsh intake of breath and slowly removed her hand, crossing her arms over her chest. "Oh, it's *Brian* now?" I clenched my jaw, staying resolute. "And how *dare* you tell me to shut up." If she seemed angry before, it was nothing like this. A closed-eyed, quiet burn. "You've *always* treated me like I'm stupid. Like you're *so* much better than me. And I've put up with it, because I'm your friend and that's just what friends are supposed to do. But you know what? I've had it. With all your lying and ignoring me and now with your dumb-ass decisions. You know what you are, Alyssa Kessler? You are a *terrible* person and a fucking failure of a friend."

It was all true so there was nothing to deny. In the midst of my own self-absorption, I had always taken Hayley for granted and furthermore, for the last three months I used her as a walking alibi to shield my actions from my parents. I looked away, too ashamed to even look her in the eye. "I'm sorry." I said.

She didn't respond initially, pretending to be concerned with her nail beds when she was really sniffing and regaining her composure. "Look, I'm just worried about you, okay? This has to stop!"

Suddenly a freshman entered the bathroom, and, seemingly unconcerned about us, went about her business in front of one of the mirrors. Hayley and I both relaxed our tense positions, but I still couldn't look at her. "Can you please give me a chance to explain, though? I can call you once classes are out today, and I'll tell you everything, I *swear*." Hayley didn't seem on board with my suggestion. "Just don't say anything, *please*." The plea was pathetic, my voice weak with holding back tears.

Shuffling her feet, Hayley shot a look back at the freshman touching up her lipgloss, then turned back at me. "I have to get to lab," she said flatly, and, hooking her hands into the straps of her backpack, hurried back out into the hallway with her head down.

I took a couple deep breaths, trying to focus on steadying my heartbeat, trying to regain my center. But the growing sound of students in the hallway and the ocean-like roar of panic in my head prevented me from doing so. The uncertainty of Hayley's next move made it so that there was no calming down, and I was drowning for a few seconds. My next exhale was a sob, ugly and clawing its way out of my throat. It was loud enough to concern the poor girl at the mirror, and I suppose it was out of sympathy that she cleared the bathroom.

There was no way I could stay in that corner forever; whether my nerves could handle it or not, I was due in the library for the exam that I was now poorly prepared for. The heels of my hands were a pitiable substitute for a tissue, and my tears were slow to dry. But after a couple minutes, I had managed to arrest a full breakdown and make myself presentable enough to make the public passage.

It seemed that more time had passed than I originally thought. I was the last of the Spanish IV students to arrive, and all but one of the partitioned desks was taken. Brian was leaning over Paco, patting his shoulder and offering some last minute advice to my rightfully-nervous fellow student. Something Paco said must have amused him greatly, because as he looked up at me his face was full of mirth. His smile dropped, however, when he took in my countenance. There was no way I could hide the tears in my eyes, and his concern became apparent very quickly. He made a twitching movement, as if he wanted to abandon the façade and rush over to comfort me, but common sense stopped him at the last minute. Brian settled instead for a tilted head, a silent question.

I wished I could have answered with a reassuring smile, but it would have only brought him peace when there should only be an absence of it. He was right to be concerned. I shook my head, an indicator to leave it alone.

* * *

I DON'T REMEMBER MUCH OF Brian's final words of encouragement before he took his leave of the library. I wasn't even paying attention as the woman administering the exam gave us instructions on what to expect during the multiple choice section. It seemed almost out of the blue that a pair of headphones appeared on my desk and we were being instructed to begin and press play on the CD players that were situated in each of our partitions.

My head swam as a long dialogue started flowing in my ears and swirling around in my brain. What the hell was I listening to? Was this Spanish? I pressed pause and leaned over the desk, head in my hands, disregarding the confused looks that were being thrown in my direction from other students down the row. I tried to control my breathing and my wayward thoughts. Would Hayley keep her promise? By the look on her face as she turned away from me, I knew that answer was no.

Before I could even entertain the idea of what would follow, I circumvented the inevitable panic by reassuring myself of one thing: Whatever happened, it wouldn't affect how Brian and I felt about each other, that we would make it through somehow. This was my lifeline; this was my focus. "It will be okay. It will be okay. Todo será bien." I whispered to myself.

Cogs clicked into place and slowly everything in my

brain switched back into Spanish mode. My preparations and study sessions came flooding back to me. A couple of breaths more and I was ready to sit up, press play, and plough into the listening portion of the exam.

Before I knew it, the section was completed, and soon I was reading, soon I was writing, soon I was speaking. One after the other, and a glance at the clock told me that despite how short a span it seemed to me, the time had been flying by at an alarming rate. I pressed the record button and rattled off the two minute presentation that capped off the entire exam. I barely had a moment to sit back in my chair and relax when the timer for the final portion rang.

Sancho whooped and hollered in celebration of the exams' end, but everyone else seemed absolutely shell-shocked. It had been a whirlwind, a year's worth of lessons and practices crammed into a three and a half month span, and suddenly it was all over.

The respite was brief. I started shrugging on my jacket, eager to get out of the classroom both because I had the rest of the school day off and I had a public bus to catch. Also, the focus that the exam had brought me was now starting to wear off and the anxiety that had gripped me before the library started to creep back in on me again like a tide.

It just so happened that Brian's lunch break

coincided with our last half hour, and he had slipped in when I wasn't looking and was catching a quick word with each of the students on their way out of the door. Pedro and Yolanda had already escaped, both looking rather downcast, and my face didn't brighten the lineup. As I approached him his face was one of cordiality, but his voice had an edge to it. "How did it go? Is everything okay?" His volume was being carefully controlled.

I shook my head, answering as low as I could. "Hayley figured it out. She knows."

He maintained composure, but he had paled considerably and one hand swiped through his dark hair in an unconscious manner. "What?" It was a declaration of confusion rather than an actual question.

There wasn't any time for me to reply before Sancho launched himself into our midst. "Señor Brown! It's over, man!" He clapped his hand loudly against Brian's back and instantly became the center of attention.

We made brief eye-contact, knowing we would finish the discussion later, and I used the interruption to disappear into the hallway.

diecinueve

THIRTY MINUTES LATER I CROSSED the threshold of my house, and all I wanted to do was to clear my head, regroup my thoughts, and find my inner peace. There was no need to panic, I told myself, until I had spoken with Brian and we laid out a plan of action. A shower seemed just the thing to do that, and while the house was still empty, I took advantage of the hot water.

Unfortunately, instead of being calming, the shower only served to remove any other distractions from my mind and I ended up staring blankly at the bottom of the bathtub, rivulets of water pooling up and rolling over my feet on their way to the drain. I could feel the dread settling like a lump in my throat. Swallowing thickly, I closed my eyes and uttered out a silent prayer. *God, please just let us get out of this okay.*

By the time my mother got home, I was dressed and a little beside myself. My face remained passive as I asked her for the keys to her car, but if she would have looked harder she would have noticed how I kept flipping my cell phone over and over in my hand to expel my nervous energy. Luckily she didn't, and she was too busy balancing her checkbook to really ask where I was going.

I was in the sedan and halfway out of Lynn Creek when my cell buzzed next to my leg where it was lying. Hayley's picture stared up at me from the display screen, and I frowned down at it before I turned my attention back to the road. I promised I would talk to her. I promised I would explain. But now wasn't the time. I needed Brian's wisdom, and together we needed to find our footing. Knowing this didn't stop my stomach from churning in guilt when I heard her call transfer to my voicemail.

The afternoon had grown considerably darker, and the proximity to the waters of Dukwibal Bay also brought about low lying clouds that rolled in from some distant ocean storm. Brian's truck was in the driveway, and I parked my sedan on the side of the street, slamming the door and approaching the white house in a rush to escape some imaginary danger. He must have heard me coming, because I barely had time to knock before the door opened to me and I was pulled in.

In the darkness of the entryway I could register only the harshest features of his face, and as I opened my mouth to say something I was suddenly silenced by hands cupping my chin and a body backing me up against the wooden frame. Brian was kissing me hungrily, desperately, as if he would never be sated, as if he would never be able to again. After the initial shock, I kissed him back, wanting so badly to lose myself in the moment. There was a threat looming over us, though, that tinged the entire encounter with a sadness that I couldn't quite put a finger on.

We surfaced for air and he backed away slowly, watching me as I regained my senses and shrugged my jacket off. "How are you?" He asked quietly.

I sighed, my hands shaking from pent up stress as I hung up my outer layer on the rack. "I..." A rumble of frustration escaped my throat. "I'm not okay. I should have known that this would happen. Hayley put two and two together when she saw your truck this morning and it wa..."

"My truck?"

"Yeah, your truck." I replied, storming into his living room. Positioning myself on one end of the couch, I watched as Brian came around as well, hovering near me but choosing not to sit. "This last Saturday she saw me getting in a truck and she asked me what was going on and I should have said something at the time..."

"Wait, what?" He seemed anxious to say something else as well, but when I continued my pent-up monologue, he settled into pacing.

"It was a mistake to use her as an excuse for where I was going. I should have known that eventually my parents would go calling her, and even though she covered for me, it was only a matter of time until she figured it out. And when she confronted me about us this morning, I handled it so poorly. I... uh, *god*!" I wasn't looking at him anymore, only at my hands lying limply in my lap. The words had been swirling around in my head all afternoon, and now as they were being said the latent feeling of self-loathing floated to the surface. "She hasn't said anything yet, but she is *so* right. I am a terrible friend. I can't believe I've been so stupid." I covered my face in my hands.

The sound of shuffling feet stopped. "We've," He corrected. "*We've* been stupid."

"What do we do now?" I asked, voice coming out muffled from between my fingers. He would know what to do, how to best approach Hayley, what to expect, how to lead us out of our predicament. My faith in him was unshakable.

Seconds passed by without a word.

If it wasn't for the sound of our breathing, I would have sworn that he had left the room. Removing the veil from my view, I took a peek to see where he was. Brian was standing where I left him, and he was staring at me with a crestfallen intensity, hand obscuring his mouth. Time expanded between us, and a silent foreboding seemed to fill the space, worming its way into every corner. My air was running out. When he finally spoke, his voice was low and even. "This needs to stop."

I blinked, trying to process, trying to find a way to breathe. "You mean we need to lie low for a while. Wait for everything to blow over, right?" When he didn't answer me, averted my gaze, I pressed him again. "*Right*?"

"You misunderstand me, Alyssa." Brian said. He brought his focus back to me, and when I saw the red rimming the brown eyes that I came to know so intimately, I felt my heart starting to break. "We can't do this anymore. We can't..." His voice cracked, but he was soon in control again. "We can't be together anymore."

And then I was suffocating.

My vision dimmed briefly as my body decided against my will that blacking out was the best way to preserve itself, shelter my heart from any more harm. I counteracted this by taking the first breath in what must have been a very long time, because the room was suddenly sharp again. Brian's voice fought for purchase along with the sound of my frantic heartbeat in my ears. I shook my head and willed myself to hear him amidst the roar.

"I've been selfish. I realize that now." Brian continued, not unmoved by my apparent distress. "Every line I crossed I justified, and every warning flag I ignored. I wanted what I wanted and I didn't ever think about what this would have meant for you if we were discovered," He laughed bitterly. "What do you think will happen to your exam results and the credits for your last two courses if they think that our relationship affected my ability to grade you fairly? You won't graduate, you won't be attending Berkeley."

I looked away.

He continued. "It would ruin your life. All for a man that you may not even want in a few years' time. You think you know yourself, Alyssa, but you really don't. Your life is just starting, and everything is changing for you. And here I am, happily blinding myself..." His sentence trailed off, the groan of frustration that followed inwardly directed. In the corner of my eye he looked ready to fly apart at the seams, but instead he swiftly kicked the coffee table that separated us and stormed into the kitchen.

The paralysis that had its hold on me while he was speaking wore off as soon as cupboard doors started slamming in the other room. The devastation that was threatening to overtake me was replaced with a growing anger. This wasn't how it was supposed to happen. Why wasn't he fighting for us? I wiped at my eyes, and displaced myself from the couch to follow after him. It all seemed so surreal, and I refused to accept the fact that he was willing to throw us away so quickly. I refused to let the hurt fully seep in. Not yet.

He had fished down a bottle of amber liquid from a top shelf and was searching for a clean glass when I got to him. "Where the hell is this coming from?" I demanded, and he set down the items in his hands and leaned on the counter, averting my eyes. His guilty demeanor spurred me on. "None of this was a problem before. We had agreed *together*!" When he still didn't answer, I attempted to reach out to him. When my hand drew close, however, he backed away from the counter and put some space between us, head still bowed. It felt as if I had been stabbed, and despite my obstinate temper still burning through me, I couldn't help but whimper.

"You didn't know what you were agreeing to. I knew, but I did it anyway." Brian said matter-of-factly, as if this was obvious, as if every word that came out of his mouth wasn't hurting me more and more.

Fight, dammit! I was losing control of my ability to think clearly in the face of his surrender, and the words started pouring out of me before I could even process them. "What about what you said about being there with me when I finally see the world? What about all that bullshit about us finding our 'normal'?" It tasted like poison on my lips, but I was too wounded to care. "White roses, new beginnings, and so, so much *bullshit*! Does that mean nothing to you now?"

My blows were well-placed, and Brian finally looked up. It was clear that he was every bit destroyed as I was. "Believe me, Alyssa," he said, voice low and gravelly and full of emotion. "There will come a day when you will forget all about me and find a good man somewhere who will be there when the time is *right*, and if you ever see me again, you will be thankful that I saved you from making a decision that you were too young to make."

In an instant, all of my confidence was obliterated, and all the wounds that my insecurity had created, the ones that he had helped heal, were torn open. The sob that escaped my mouth was a reflex, and angry, unbidden tears were spilling over my lashes. "How can you say something like that?" I hated my voice, how small it sounded. "You were the one who trusted in my abilities more than anyone else I had ever met and now you're telling me what?" I threw my hands in the air. "That you were *mistaken*? Do you have no trust in me at all? In *us*?"

"No, Alyssa. I..."

"That you *lied* to me?"

What I had just said hung in the air between us, and immediately I wished I could take it back. It wasn't true and I knew it. He pinched the bridge of his nose between his thumb and forefinger. He was trying not to cry as well. "Brian," I started, wanting to plead, wanting to apologize.

"I don't trust *myself*," He said quietly, as if I wasn't meant to hear it.

I sniffed, trying to silence myself, not entirely sure of what I heard. "What?"

Brian gave up on his self-imposed distance, and he crossed the divide. His hand hesitated before reaching up to wipe away the salty tears from my cheek with the pad of his thumb. He looked down on me, conflicted, fingers lingering on the back of my neck. His voice was nearly a whisper now, but it was directed at me. "You were mistaken to trust me." He couldn't hide the sorrow in his voice anymore, not with the physical connection making it so real, too real. "You followed my lead because you didn't know better and I failed to give a damn about the consequences to you and your future. I've been rudely awakened and it's time now to put an end to this. *Because I love you*." He leaned down and kissed my hair, and when he withdrew, he took his person, his promises, and our possible future with him. "I'm only sorry it took me this long."

Within a few minutes time, all of my hopes were dashed, and the man standing across from me had transformed from my lover back into a stranger.

I felt like screaming, tearing, pleading...

...but I couldn't bring myself to do any of those things.

I couldn't bring myself to do anything.

My despair had numbed me, paralyzed me. Only my eyes seemed to still function as I blinked furiously, shedding the tears that congregated, persisting to blur my vision. After a long moment I finally was able to inhale, the air intolerably thick. I choked back another sob, swallowed it down.

Brian... no, it was Mr. Brown now, hesitated, his eyes mercurial and full of regret. There was a visible twitch in his arms, and I vainly hoped that he would give into it and embrace me again, take it all back. But instead, he redirected this errant energy into a staggered walk over to the entry way, taking my jacket off of its hook. "Blame it all on me, Alyssa." He murmured, back to me. "Whatever it takes for you to move forward. Hate me, if you must."

My brow furrowed, and I stared at a spot on the floor just clear of his figure in the doorway. "I could never do that." I insisted, but my voice was weak, unconvincing.

It was by no small feat that I found myself moving, reaching, exiting the open door that had somehow appeared in front of me. Outside the clouds had disappeared, and the bay stretched itself out into the distance, gray suggestions of islands dotting the horizon. The wind carried up the hill and crashed upon me, its fingers dragging icily up my spine. I shivered, jacket hanging uselessly from my fingertips.

And in my spare moment of distraction, the door had clicked behind me, and I was left alone. The sound of it caused me to turn around, and I contemplated the heaviness of the wood, the realness of its barrier. Somewhere on the other side, I heard something crashing, something being destroyed.

We were more like Manuel and Isabel than we realized, I thought, shuddering in the cold and listening to my teacher's muffled grief.

Things were never meant to end happily for us.

Like so many Spanish tales, our story was always bound for tragedy.

veinte

THE DRIVE HOME WAS A blur.

Despite what I had said only moments ago, I found myself blinded by an all-pervasive hate. Any of it directed at Brian, however, was quickly cut off, shoved down, denied.

It was myself I hated.

I had made this happen.

I had let this happen.

What had started as a tickle in the back of my brain, an idle fancy of a teenager's mind, had turned into full blown action. I had chosen to step over that line. Maybe Brian was right. Who was I to imagine myself in love?

In real, proper love?

But then again, a little voice reminded me, *who was he to take advantage of that misappropriated love? I'm not the only one to blame here...*

"Goddammit!" I screamed, pounding my fists on the steering wheel. I refused to let that line of thinking take me over, letting the persistent ache in the center of my chest, the pain of my fingernails digging into unyielding plastic be the proof of what I knew was true.

This had been real.

My love had been *real*.

And so had his.

* * *

WHEN I BURST THROUGH THE living room, interrupting my parents' news program, it was clear by my red face and haphazard movement that I was in distress.

But now wasn't the time to explain anything to them.

Never was the time to explain to them.

I tossed the car keys in the direction of the hooks on the wall, not even stopping to watch them hit the plaster and crash upon the hardwood floor.

"Alyssa!" My dad shouted after me from his seat. Whether his tone was in response to my careless action or if it was actual concern for my mental state, I didn't turn around to find out.

I slipped into my bedroom, and for the first time in memory, I used the lock on my door.

✴ ✴ ✴

I WOKE UP THE NEXT day, unnaturally exhausted, an hour still until my alarm rang for school that day. Staring up at the ceiling, eyes crusted with the salt of tears that had been shed in my fitful sleep, I contemplated skipping.

Skipping the day.

Skipping the week.

Skipping the month.

Skipping town.

How could I go back to what my life was before? How could I pretend that nothing had ever happened?

One thing I did know, though: Whatever I felt, despite how much I wanted to run from everything, retreat was not an option. To take Brian's grand gesture, to waste the opportunity that he gave me to succeed and prosper, would be the ultimate sin. It would be spitting on his desire for me to thrive.

Even if that means thriving without him, I thought, swallowing thickly. My eyes blurred with the threat of fresh tears, and I blinked furiously.

It was a war with leaden limbs to get myself out of bed, get myself dressed, search for my notebooks and assignments. Go through the motions.

Upon emerging from my bedroom, I could hear the clinking of cups that told me that my parents were in the kitchen preparing their ritual coffee. Unwilling to pass by them on my way out, I opted for the back door.

The latch of the garden gate clicked behind me, and I sought the silence of the early morning. The sound of birds, the quiet wind, and the feel of dew soaking through the canvas of my shoes acting as my focal points, my link to peace.

Breathe, I told myself. *One class, and then the next, and then the next. Everything will be fine.* It was a lie I was telling myself, I knew, but I willed it to be true. There was still a chance that this was still all a terrible nightmare, and somehow if I played along I would suddenly come to from my coma and everything would be alright.

A wayward breath of cool air tickled my face and ushered me forward, starting my reluctant trek toward

Lynn Creek High School.

* * *

HAYLEY WAS MYSTERIOUSLY ABSENT FROM Physics that morning, but that seemed about the only thing that registered in my depressed state. The conversation of the students around me I easily tucked away in the corner of my mind, ignored and eclipsed by the roar of my dark and formless thoughts. My body sat obediently through the first three periods, an impulse, an auto-pilot. It was almost by surprise that I blinked and found myself walking down that hallway, into that courtyard.

My anxiety kicked back in, causing my heart to pound uncomfortably as I took in that metal door. It was only as recent as two days ago that we were kissing each other just behind that door, safe and sheltered in the dark... I closed my eyes against that memory, shaking my head.

For a few minutes I was glued to my spot, lingering outside the entrance. I had managed to bring myself here, and yet my resolve had crumbled at the thought of entering Mr. Brown's classroom. There was a fear to enter and find myself alone once more with him, raw and at a loss of what to say. So like the coward I was, I waited and watched as several of my classmates entered ahead. Finally, as I felt I had created enough of a buffer, I laid hold of the handle and stepped inside.

Mr. Brown was not yet present in the classroom. Yolanda and Katalina were happily chatting details about the upcoming prom, an event that I had cared so little about that I had forgotten all about it. Katalina was sitting backwards on her desk top, sandaled feet resting on the connected seat. Her back was to me as I unloaded my math assignment and sat down.

"Hey, Julietta!"

I blinked in confusion and looked away from my work to see Sancho regarding me from across the row. I couldn't remember him ever initiating a conversation with me before, but his face looked honest, so I tried to respond. "Yeah?" My voice was rusty.

Sancho leaned a little in my direction. "How do you think you did on the exam yesterday?"

There was a moment where I was completely lost but then I remembered.

Ah, yes.

The exam.

Somewhere in the middle of my emotional trauma I had actually sat through the advanced placement exam. My quietness seemed to concern Sancho, because he seemed about ready to comment on it.

"Oh, you know she passed it." Katalina offered flippantly, not caring to turn around and face us. Her hand waved over her shoulder, lazily indicating me. "When does she not?"

I grimaced as she turned her attention back to her own conversation, unsure if I should be flattered or offended by the jealousy-tinged compliment that she threw in my direction.

The door opened behind us and I tensed in expectation. The voices of Paco and Pedro floated into the room however and I was left shaking with the false alarm. My head hit the desk and I tried to force myself to breathe normally.

Luckily Sancho was not observing my behavior. "¿Qué tal, mis hermanos?" He shouted at them as they found their seats. There was an onslaught of friendly roughhousing and I was quickly forgotten.

About thirty seconds later, the final bell for 4th period rang and there was some shuffling as the boys picked themselves up off the floor and Katalina repositioned herself properly in her seat. A silence descended as we waited for Mr. Brown to enter. I closed my eyes briefly and issued a silent prayer.

And we waited.

We waited silently for one minute, and when he still

had not entered, the idle chatter started up again.

Another two minutes passed.

"I say we ditch," Paco's suggestion was accompanied by a smirk.

Pedro kept his eye on the door. "Brown *is* here today, right?"

Yolanda looked up from the cellphone that she had fished out of her backpack. "Yeah, he is. Something's wrong with him, though."

I stared blankly at my desk.

The entire class' interest was piqued. "What do you mean, *wrong*?" asked Katalina.

Yolanda set her phone down and clarified. "Yeah, so Cherity has Spanish II during second period and she says that they were given worksheets and he didn't say anything for, like, the *entire* period." Someone scoffed, and Yolanda sucked in air through her teeth. "Seriously though," the volume of her voice lowered, and there was a collective rustling and bodies were leaned in her direction. "I was passing by the staff lounge and the other teachers were talking about it, too. They're all worried about him. He's practically catatonic or something."

I covered my mouth with my hands and tried to remain as still as possible. My insides were quivering with grief, my heart reaching out, sensing the pain that my other half was in and feeling it blend with my own. He had not even entered the room yet and this was already beginning to be more than I could take.

The conversation continued on behind me. "Do you think it's like a girlfriend problem? Wasn't he dating someone?"

"I think so. It's not like he volunteers personal details about his love life in class or anything."

"Yo, Alyssa," Pedro's voice was aimed at the back of my head. "You talk to him more than any of us do. Has he ever mentioned a girlfriend?"

I was saved from producing a response, because the classroom door opened and the topic of our conversation finally entered. His familiar footsteps hesitated before they resumed a pace that slowly was bringing him to the front of the classroom. I struggled to keep my head down, not trusting my face to remain passive if I dared to face him, make eye contact.

"Definitely a girlfriend," Katalina whispered to Yolanda.

Despite my best interest, my eyes betrayed me and flitted up to his face as he passed. My stomach sunk at the sight of his drained pallor and the harsh line of his mouth. When he approached the podium, I could see his head very carefully swivel across the room, and I knew he was deliberately keeping me out of his gaze. Straight ahead of me, I could see his hand reach out, a tremor manifesting as he gripped the edges of his podium for support.

Why are you doing this, Brian? I wanted to undo all this, undo what had happened and just comfort him, erase his unnecessary suffering.

But...

After a brief moment my thoughts turned bitter. I reminded myself that this was all brought on by his own action, that this was supposedly for my own good. I frowned, hating myself for thinking this way, but finding that it was soon becoming all I could focus on. I directed the disgust toward both of us in equal measure, fostering it into full-bloom, the anger preferable to the sadness that was previously tearing me apart.

"Good afternoon, class." Mr. Brown dispensed with the Spanish, a testament to his altered state.

"Dude, we weren't *that* bad yesterday, were we?" Paco asked.

Our teacher slow-blinked, and took in a deep breath while contemplating the floor. When his face resurfaced, it seemed more tranquil. "No, you weren't. In fact, given the short amount of time that we had to prepare, I'm pretty pleased with how you guys performed. I'm proud of you."

He made eye contact with every student in the room, with the exception of me.

"Aw, yeah. We're the best. ¡Somos los mejores!" commented Sancho, turning around to high-five Paco behind him.

Despite himself, Mr. Brown's mouth twitched in a small smile.

The classroom door opened and Brown's attention was immediately drawn to who walked through it, jaw clenched tightly. Every student turned around to see the Principal, Mr. Farnsworth, standing alongside a short, balding man that I didn't recognize holding a briefcase. I was filled with a sense of dread.

For his part, Mr. Farnsworth looked livid, his barely maintained calm causing a tic that made his reddish mustache shudder. He addressed Brian directly. "I need to speak to you in my office immediately."

I didn't hear any movement from behind me. Brian wasn't moving.

Farnsworth gestured to the man next to him. "Mr. Pataki here will substitute for you in your absence."

Not a one of my classmates made a noise. They could sense the gravity of the situation, and a couple of us, myself included, turned to see Mr. Brown's reaction.

There was no way to hide the fear in my eyes, I knew. Briefly, very briefly, Brian sought my face, and there was no mistaking the regret, the apology he tried to convey to me in that split second. He looked back up at the Principal. "Sure. Sure." He was distracted, but his was a voice of resignation. He released his grip on the podium, hands still shaking even as they formed fists and pressed to his sides. A breeze stirred up as he passed, and my heart ached, yearning to leap out of my chest and follow behind him.

Mr. Farnsworth held the door open as Mr. Brown went before him. He shot us an appraising look before pulling up the rear, letting the door fall closed. Through the window, we saw their figures pass through the courtyard. Then we were alone with a nervous-looking Mr. Pataki.

The substitute teacher was quickly ignored, and he barely had any time to contain the class before protests and mutterings of concern flooded the entire group.

"What was that all about?"

"Is Mr. Brown in trouble?"

"Man, that did not look good. That didn't look good at *all*."

"Farnsworth is *pissed*, bro."

Mr. Pataki cleared his throat, attempting to get the

class back under control, but he was clearly out of his depth. "If everyone can be quiet for just one second..."

I closed my eyes briefly, trying to sort out my thoughts. It was clear that Brian had been found out, and it was safe to say that my name had come up too. It was only a matter of time before I was called out as well. The ship was sinking fast and my only thought was to stem the flow of water, no matter how hopeless it seemed.

Whatever was being thrown at him, I knew it couldn't be the whole truth. Crude accusations were going to be thrown at him, and there was going to be no way for him to defend himself. My voice may not matter, but I had to try at least. In the midst of the continuing chatter, I raised my hand.

Pataki seemed relieved that someone was following protocol. "Yes, Miss...?" The poor man searched for my name, having been dropped there with no information to guide him.

"Kessler," I provided, not leaving any space for his acknowledgment before I started speaking again. "Can I be excused? I need to go to the bathroom."

The substitute shook his head. "Class only started. There's no reason for you to..."

"I *need* to leave, sir." My panic added a hard edge to my voice, daring him to say no again.

"Now, if you really need to use the bathroom, you should have done so before..."

I was tired of the formality and couldn't be bothered with any more roadblocks. I grabbed my backpack and, not looking back, pushed my way through the aisle packed with student bodies leaning into each other with their loud gossip.

"Miss Kessler!"

His shout was cut short by the slamming of the classroom door. I crossed the empty courtyard and entered the main hallway, making short time of the distance to the office. If I could get there before allegations were made, perhaps I could say something...

At the end of the fluorescent-lit hallway, I saw a blonde figure exit through the office door. When I realized who it was, I started running.

"Hayley!"

She flinched at my voice, and when she turned to face me I could see that she was visibly upset. When I got closer though, her expression was quickly covered with a mask of derision. "I'm sorry. I had to."

It would have been in my best interest to apologize, I knew, for failing to answer her call last night, for failing to call her back. *Too late now*, my addled mind whispered to me. I was already paying dearly for it. "What did you do?"

I asked weakly.

Hayley initially avoided eye-contact, perhaps out of guilt. "Mr. Brown had to be reported. It was necessary." She looked back at me, resolve wavering. "Don't worry, I didn't give them your name."

She had reported Brian with no specifics. I saw a break in the clouds and felt the knot on my heart lessen. Without my name and my authentication, there was nothing the district could use against him. There was only a reported rumor from a dubious source.

But the next few words shattered any peace that may have settled on me. "I don't know what your parents will do, though."

"My...?" The words wouldn't leave my throat unaccompanied by a fresh track of tears. "My parents?" Now I knew why Hayley was absent this morning. I was horrified. If Hayley didn't give my name, they certainly would.

Hayley was biting her lip, watching the emotions take hold of my small frame. She looked ready to say something, perhaps she was starting to regret her decisions, but I didn't give her the chance. I pushed past her and aimed for the exit. Brian could hold his own against Hayley's allegations, but I was more concerned now about what would happen if my parents stepped forward, if they hadn't already.

Everything was going to hell around me, and all I could do was run for home as fast as my legs could carry me.

veintiuno

BY THE TIME I APPROACHED the house, I was out of breath and beyond a reasonable state of anxiety. Not knowing what to expect, I braced myself and, with shaking hands, unlocked the front door.

The conversation on the other side stopped as soon as the hinges creaked.

I looked around the door.

My parents were both in the living room. They had ceased whatever they were doing and were now frozen, their penetrating stares directed toward me. Dad had obviously been pacing, and a flush was starting to creep up his neck. Mom was leaning forward in the wing-back chair, cradling what must have been not her first cup of coffee. It looked cold, though, and her right foot was fidgeting idly to dispel some nervousness. The glare of their shell-shocked eyes made me stop dead in my tracks. In all my rush to get home, I had failed to prepare myself with any words to say.

Dad was the first to speak. "Is it true?" he asked thickly, his look conveying dismay and disbelief at the same time.

I gave myself a moment to gather my thoughts by setting my bag down and closing the door quietly behind me. By the time I turned back around and settled myself on the floral couch, I felt more composed. "Depends on what you were told," I answered cautiously. There was no knowing exactly what Hayley said to them.

Mom made a snorting noise, but remained silent otherwise. Dad continued to steer the conversation. "Hayley showed up this morning and claimed that you have been lying about where you've been going on Saturdays. She says that you haven't been to her house in months."

It was hard to read my parents' expressions. But it was clear that this was the first of many questions. The tip of the iceberg. The chance for me to redeem myself and come clean before the jury was at hand, but like the weakling I was, I didn't take it. The longer path to truth was riddled with uncomfortable questions, but it seemed safer. "No, I haven't," I admitted.

Everything was drawn up tight like a string on a bow; one more question would set the arrow flying. The air seemed to vibrate with the tension as my father spoke his carefully chosen words. "Alyssa, Hayley seems to think that you have become inv-v..." He seemed embarrassed, tripping over the word. "...*Involved* with a teacher." His pale eyes bored into mine and I had to look away. "Is it true?"

My silence was the greatest witness, confirming the truth before I was even able to speak up for myself. I kept my eyes on the leg of the coffee table, concentrating on maintaining an even tone to my voice. "If you let me explain," I said as coolly as I could, "it's not what it looks like..."

The arrow released and the verdict was in.

My mother opened her mouth the first time since I set foot in the house. "Not what it looks like!?" Her volume was dangerously high. "You've been sneaking around behind our backs and sleeping around with a teacher! What is that *supposed* to look like?"

My reaction to her acidic words was instantaneous. I leapt to my feet, shivering in anger. "If that's what you think I've been doing, then I'm sorry you have such poor confidence in me!"

"Clearly, though, I'm in the right, considering your behavior!"

I tried to backpedal. "It's not what it looks like." I said again, slowing my words for emphasis. "I was not sleeping with him. Yes, I was in a relationship with him, but he respects me."

My mom stood up, now agitated and pacing, and my dad took her place in the wing-back chair. He was still solemn and thoughtful, trying his best not to lose his temper. "It may seem like that to you," he agreed, "But anyone who would take advantage of his position of authority over you can't have honorable intentions. It would have been only a matter of time..."

Fighting the urge to cry, I covered my face with my hands for a few seconds, physically blocking out what my father was suggesting. "It doesn't matter now, anyway," I said. "I'm not even seeing him anymore, and I won't tell you his name." I flashed what I hoped was a defiant look in my mother's direction. "I won't have you calling the school and jeopardizing his job. He hasn't *done* anything!"

Dad threw his hand on his hip, looking at me pointedly in a way that instantly made me feel like I was five years old again. "Calm down, Alyssa."

I sat back down.

He continued. "Oddly enough, I believe you. Plus

you're a horrible liar when you're upset. I would have been able to tell." He saw by the thin line of my mouth that I was trying very hard to remain silent, so he answered my unspoken question. "Your mother and I already discussed it and we're not going to say anything to the school. You're extremely close to graduation and having your name associated with any scandal involving a teacher will possibly jeopardize your possibility of getting your diploma."

I frowned, letting out a sigh of simultaneous relief and frustration. "Thank you," I said quietly.

"That's not putting aside the fact that we are deeply, *deeply* disappointed in you, Alyssa," He added. "We thought we raised you to be smarter than this. Your mother and I..."

"Yes!" My mom chimed in, turning back around mid-pace. She clanked her useless cup of coffee on the table, leaning over it and into my space. "You never gave a thought of how this could have all come crashing down around our heads! If this had gotten out, the entire town would have thought that I had raised a..." She fished for what I could only assume was the most hurtful word she could imagine. "That we had raised a little whore!"

She was inches away from me. Her words caused me to recoil, my resolve starting to crumble. Yet I refused to break eye contact with her. "It would have been a pity to stain your perfect reputation, *Mother*," I commented sourly.

Something flashed across her face, and for a brief second I thought that I was going to receive a slap for my remark. But at the last moment she pulled away from me, standing back up to her full height. As soon as she gave me purchase I got back to my feet and we both retreated to opposite sides of the room, me backing toward an exit and she toward the safety of my father. She turned her back to me, leaning toward him for comfort. He smoothed his hand down her arm in an attempt to assuage her, but as he was watching me in a puzzled manner, trying to figure me out, his effort was distracted and half-hearted.

"How did we let this happen?" my mother asked, maybe to my father, maybe to no one in particular. "How could we have not seen this?"

At that moment, something snapped within me. There was no thought-process that seemed to proceed; my response was primal, a blind lashing out against bonds that I refused to endure any longer. "Let this happen? *Let this happen?!*" I took a few steps back in her direction, and she turned to face me. "There was no *you* letting any of this happen. I chose my own actions." I bared my teeth in disgust, letting my voracious need to vent feed my words. "And if maybe you had been a little less concerned about my grades, my useless performance record, and more concerned with learning about *who I am* as a *person*, then maybe you would have figured it out. Maybe you would have seen it. But you've never asked. You never cared. As it is, you've had your head up your ass this entire time!"

I barely registered the numbed, shocked face of my mother before I took my leave, feeling justly satisfied. It was only after the slam of my bedroom door that I heard my mother start crying, and the sound broke through my adrenaline. I sunk to the floor against the wall, feeling instant remorse.

It wasn't supposed to be this way. None of it.

I pulled my knees up to my chest, resting my chin on top of my knees, feeling the tears begin. They seemed to be my cruel companion now, always present, no deliverance in sight. I began slipping down the familiar slope to depression, letting myself wallow in self-pity.

Scattered across my room were the remnants of the previous night's despair. The comforter for my bed was now on the floor, kicked there by fitful sleep. Books were piled on the floor near the bookcase, tossed there carelessly in an attempt to procure what was stashed among them. My eyes locked on the offending journal, splayed open to reveal its contents, its pages polluted with the ink of Spanish prose. I had poured over those pages last night, drowning in the melancholy of Marquez, of Esquivel, of Allende. Using them as balm like a drunk would use whiskey. From my vantage point I could see the lovesick stanzas of Carmen Marín on the open page:

'Yo soy de mi amado, y él es mio,' ('I am my beloved's and my beloved is mine.')

Las palabras de la Santa Biblia (The words of the Holy Bible)

Palabras que se escondían de mi corazón... (Words that were hidden from my heart...)

Hasta que apareció tu cara. (Until your face appeared.)

Y ahora, (And now)

Ahora comprendo esta frase eterna. (And now I understand that eternal phrase.)

I hated those words. I hated the journal that I had penned with such longing, such naiveté. Reaching forward across the messy floor, I snatched up the paper-bound hopes and dreams and held them in my hands, feeling the weight of them. Then, with a feeling of sick pleasure, I started to rip out the pages, rip those pages in half. Half-baked came the idea that perhaps I should burn the remains as well. But I knew it wasn't going to be enough. There was nothing I could do to erase the pain and failure of this whole situation. I pressed my fists into the carpet, letting my emotions bubble up and escape from my mouth as a strangled scream.

Heavy breathing eased into a calmer state, my form huddled among the mangled remains of the hated journal. With a clearer mind, I was reminded of the fact that eventually I would have to face the world again, face the parents that were still beside themselves in the other room. They most likely heard my meltdown, and were probably wondering if I was mentally unstable. I wondered the same thing, too.

The urge I felt that morning returned. The feeling to escape everything, to get the hell out of Lynn Creek, washed over me and filled me with conviction. Getting back to my feet, wiping at my face, I stumbled over to my desk, pushing aside flash cards and textbooks to get at what I was looking for. The packet of information emblazoned with its familiar round crest presented itself upon being unburied from a pile of essay rough drafts.

I sifted through the contents and found the application I was looking for: freshman admittance to summer classes at Berkeley. The deadline was coming up in a couple weeks, and it seemed bittersweet providence that this escape came at an opportune moment. If I could keep my head down and my resolve unwavering for one more month, I could finish the school year strong and leave this waste of a town behind. The only thing that could possibly bungle this plan was my heart. If I let it, it would bleed through the sleeve of any disguise I attempted to wear. And that was unacceptable.

From now on, I told myself, *there will be no more feeling sorry for yourself. No more falling prey to your emotions. You'll do what you have to do to get out of here. Forget Brian.*

Taking a seat at the desk, and taking a deep breath, I began to put pen to paper. The fields were filled without thought and without hesitation until my pen reached *Desired Field of Study.* My hand hovered over the paper while I fought an internal battle. In the end, even though I knew I would regret it, I decided to let my heart win out over one more thing before I locked it away. There was no way I could deny it this, no matter how painful it may be.

Desired Field of Study: Spanish

veintidos

I RAN INTO THE WATER, the waves tickling at my waist. The wind swept across the water and stung my eyes. Tears that were already starting to well up in my eyes were trickling down my cheek...

The sun dipped into the horizon, the gold and fuschia colors mingling with the water. Evening was coming on fast, yet I stood there, continuing to stare out at phantoms until the constant murmur of the crowds died away behind me. As the orb slipped into the depths of the ocean, a refreshing coolness settled in the air. The stillness on the beach accentuated every sound, the soft pattering of feet in sandals in the sand echoing...

Suddenly the silence was broken, the sound of water stirring telling me that someone was wading out into the depths, perhaps to cool off before the night came. Mesmerized, I found myself fascinated with the way the soft swishing fell into step with the silver rings. The ripples of the stranger's disturbance sailed past me, evaporating into the light.

At first I thought the person was going to pass me, that I may get a glance of this late night beach-walker. But the sloshing slowed, the final wave of movement very near to me. I felt my skin tingle with the proximity of someone so close, and I stilled my body to hear the breathing of the silent figure behind me. Something deep inside me already knew who it was, but at the moment I refused to believe it. Impossible...

I held my breath as I heard a hand moving, sensing it reaching out to touch me. Already the warmth was radiating across the expanses between our two forms. Panic took over me, and before the skin touched mine, I flipped around, ready to confront...ready to confront...

Those eyes.

Those eyes, burning with the reflection of the sunset and their own passion. They had never ceased to take my breath away as they were doing that very moment. My legs lost all feeling, the shock making me lose all rationality, rendering myself unable to catch myself as I stumbled.

But he caught me. And when I finally felt his hands grasping my waist, back where they belonged, holding me,

I woke up out of my speechlessness and whispered the first thing that came to my mind.

"Brian?"

There was no mistaking him for anyone else. This was my Brian, back from the grave, full of so much life, now standing in front of me, tangible. He smiled softly, not saying a word, but reaching up to tuck a strand of free-flying hair behind my ear, letting his fingers trail down my jaw.

I shivered. I had so much to say, and there was so much that I needed to hear. I opened my mouth, my voice coming quietly, hesitantly. "How...how did you find me?" My eyes lazily slid shut, fighting off the urge to just lose myself to the sensations, blissfully drugged.

"No matter how lost you are, Alyssa, I will always find you..."

* * *

THE SOUND OF MY OWN sobs woke me up.

I could hear the noise reverberate against the bare walls and I kept my eyes squeezed shut, wishing for the darkness that would take me back to that nonexistent beach. That beach was the only place we had left, even if it was only a cruel dream.

The real Brian wouldn't come to rescue me.

Three months later, and he hadn't even tried to call.

I rolled onto my back, brushing my hands through knotted hair and staring up at the white ceiling. I missed the stars, missed my own personal Polaris. There was no guidance to be found, no wishes to be made on the white vastness above me now.

Something had to be done about my restless sleep, I decided. It would be distinctly awkward to interrupt my roommate's slumber with my recurring nightmares. But there was nothing I knew to do to stop them. His face filled my nightly visions just like it consumed all moments of mental idleness in the day. Luckily my roommate would not be arriving for another couple weeks. Soon the empty twin bed across from me would be filled with a stranger that would likely be perturbed by my apparent mental volatility.

After a moment of concentrated breathing, I stretched out my legs and swung them over the edge of the mattress, making contact with floor and sluggishly pulling myself across the room to the window. Yanking on the cord and raising the blinds, I could see that the fog was still lingering below, clinging to the edges of the hills with smoky tendrils. San Francisco was barely discernible across the bay, the peninsula a dark blue mass barely peeking over the roofs of the buildings that obscured the full vista.

Berkeley was treating me well. The classes were challenging, and for the most part, I found myself so busy with research and essays that I hardly had any time to feel sorry for myself. It was always in the night, though, in the quiet of the morning, and on the non-structured weekends that I found myself contemplative and miserable. My depression felt like the Central Californian fog, insidious and apt to shroud everything without a moment's notice.

It had been a hell of a month, those days leading up to my graduation at Lynn Creek High School. Somehow, even without my name showing up in any official inquiry, it became a poorly kept secret amongst the students that I was willing to sleep with any teacher just to get my grade. There were snickers that erupted behind my back as I passed in the halls, and the coldness from both students and once-approving teachers had me crying in the bathroom stalls.

At home, it wasn't much better. My father pretended that nothing happened, asking about my finals and passing the salt at dinner, but in the times when he thought I wasn't looking, there was a sadness that came across his features.

My mother didn't speak to me at all. She was ashamed, I knew, but there was nothing that I could have said to fix it. Time was my only hope for a repair in our relationship.

Brian, I suppose, did the only thing that he thought he deserved. They were never able to corroborate Hayley's story, and my parents didn't step forward as promised. But it wouldn't have mattered anyway. They didn't even have a chance to interrogate him on the matter before he willingly admitted that he had crossed the line as a teacher with a student, and announced his resignation right there in the principal's office. He never came back to his classroom.

I tried to call him when I found out what had happened. It was with a fool's hope that I believed that somehow now that everything had run its course, that he would be willing to fix what had been broken. I left multiple messages on his phone, begging him to talk to me, telling him that it wasn't just his fault, only *his* burden to bear. When I didn't receive a reply, I went to bang on his door. It was only once, and the pain of knowing he was in the house, blatantly ignoring the sound of my voice on the other side of the door, was too heartbreaking to repeat. He believed too deeply in his need to protect me and hated himself too much for me to convince him otherwise. My mind wanted me to hate him, but my heart knew differently. My dreams were proof positive for that.

By the time I walked to get my diploma, I had managed to lose the respect of my peers, lose my best friend, lose the trust of my parents, and lose the man I loved. I shook the hand of Principal Farnsworth and received the symbolic paper, honor cords decorating my robe, and nobody cheered for me, save for the few polite people who didn't know of me and my exploits. Berkeley was waiting to receive me with open arms, and I was glad to run, not daring to look back.

I wondered, standing there by the window, whether or not Brian was okay. The last month of his Spanish class without him present was like attending a funeral. Although Mr. Pataki struggled to take charge of the class, the ghost of Mr. Brown still lingered in corners of the room, in the projects and posters that he had accumulated throughout the year. We all missed him. We all missed our teacher. But I felt it more keenly. Not only did I miss my teacher, I missed what felt like the other half of me. I ached for him, for his comfort, for his words of advice. I could see his face in my mind, and I could see his own sorrow, and I wished to touch his face and erase the lines I saw there.

Behind me, my phone went off, announcing a new text message. I didn't even need to check to see who it was. It was always the same person. Hayley, trying to apologize and explain her actions once again. I re-listened to her most recent voice mail the night before, where she said she felt sorry for spreading those rumors about me. She was hurting, she explained, and she had wanted to get back at me, but she regretted it now. I wasn't ready to forgive her, though. Forgiving her would come hand in hand with forgiving myself, and that was still miles away.

So there I was, isolated, nightmare-ridden and in a city that I didn't know. Any support system that I may have had was all gone, and it was all my fault. I had dared to dream, dared to break the rules in the hope of my happily ever after, and I had freely walked into the snare. The snare may have been welcoming, may have been beautiful, but it was a snare nonetheless. And I would have gladly stayed there forever. But Brian had decided that it was his responsibility to release me, that I needed to see my trap for what it really was. How fitting, I thought bitterly, that he had done so because he had wanted to protect me, wanted what was in my best interest. *You thought it was for my own good, Brian.* I shook my head, burying my face in my hands, hiding away in my own anguish. *Now we're both alone and everything fell apart anyway.*

I spent a better part of that Saturday morning crying, something that was now my modus operandi. Everything that I had tried to escape from had followed me to California in the form of grief-inducing memories and regrets. In this shape I could barely function, and I knew that if I continued to wallow in my self-indulgent unhappiness, things would never get better. *Brian wouldn't have wanted it this way,* my inner voice told me.

The cycle had to be broken. And somehow, that

morning, the time had come.

As the sun rose higher and the fog burned away, it had become clear to me that it was time to move on. I was tired of allowing myself to feel like the victim, tired of enveloping myself in my sorrow like a security blanket. Eighteen years was not enough time to write my life off forever, and the only way things were going to get better was if I stepped forward and took my future into my own hands.

I was already on the right path. Berkeley would be my saving grace, and my motivation would be furthering my education, taking advantage of the opportunities that I was now presented with. My focus would be iron-clad, and my heart wouldn't waver. I wouldn't let it. Safe in a box is where it was going to stay until my task was complete, until I was ready.

I will find a life without Brian, I declared to myself that day, *and I will find a way to forget all about him.*

Este es un día nuevo.

Today was a new day.

SIX YEARS LATER

epílogo

I HAD SENSED IT COMING for weeks now, a slow crawling of dread undercutting what should have been a sigh of relief. My Masters of Education was only lacking my thesis paper; I was *so* close. Initially, I hadn't noticed the signs, my focus being so squarely on my work. The change in Matt's behavior was nearly imperceptible, too. But still, I should have known that my impending departure from Berkeley would ignite a fire under him.

We had met at the University library. I was in search of a misplaced microfiche and he was the helpful intern who probably misplaced it. He was charming. He was sweet. More importantly, he was safe. And he liked me way more than I liked him. So I gave him a shot, and within a year that shot turned into living together and evenings of take-out Chinese and in-house lazy pants. It wasn't *apassionado*, but it was comfortable.

That night our tiny dining room table was littered with papers and index cards full of notes. I was in full-blown study mode, but I was aware of him stealing glances at me over his novel when he thought I wasn't looking. The feeling of dread crept up my throat again and I tamped it down.

"So, do you want to marry me?"

I looked up from my textbook, my face covered in shock. My initial thought process was taken up with the inappropriateness of the whole setting. Who the hell proposes in the middle of a study session? This wasn't some romantic dinner with champagne... I was wearing sweat pants with holes in them, for goodness sake.

Then the gravitas of his words finally hit me. Matt was actually *proposing to me*.

My lack of reaction made him squirm. "Maybe?" Matt amended.

The thoughts in my brain were too many to process, so my primal instinct was to retreat back to my notes. I looked away and went back to writing my abandoned paragraph.

My continued silence prompted him to scoot forward in his chair, and he slowly pried the pencil out of my hand and pushed the textbook out of the way. I huffed in frustration, but he bent toward me and brushed my lips in a kiss. "Alyssa, I love you. Please marry me."

His face was inches from mine, and with my distractions taken away from me I had no other option but to contemplate his features. By now they were so familiar to me. That look of earnestness, the blonde stubble that his upper lip would disappear into whenever he smiled, his gentle blue eyes.

Right now those pale eyes were full of hope, but when I blinked and looked again, all I could see were dark, piercing ones, and I was at once disoriented. I shook my head, trying to drown out the strong, uninvited memories that filled my mind suddenly. They descended on me, impenetrable. Enraptured me.

The warm hands that held mine.

A teasing laugh.

The scent of him, cedar soap and something always uniquely *him*...

Julietta loca...

"'Lys?"

Matt's voice brought me back to the present. I swallowed thickly, realizing that I still hadn't provided him an answer. I forced myself to focus.

Matt loved me. And I loved him. I loved Matt...

Did I love Matt?

Of course I did. I mean, just look at how comfortable we were, how easily we got along! Marriage...

...was the next logical step.

My stomach churned as the realization came crashing down and a memory of his voice rose up in me, shouting out of my past.

"Whether or not this is something I'm supposed to be doing, all I know is that I can't stand not having you in my life. I want this. I want you..."

Dammit, Brian! Let me be!

Tears blurred my vision and I gasped for breath. My old wounds were reopening, and though it hurt as freshly as it ever had, I felt awake for what seemed like the first time in years.

Reaching out, I grasped Matt's face with both of my hands, and he yielded as I bent him forward and kissed the crown of his head. "I'm sorry." My voice was low and watery. "I can't do this. You are kind, you are wonderful, and you deserve someone better than me."

Something tugged at me from deep within, as if there was a string tied to my ribcage, and some distant movement was compelling me, dragging me away from the safety of San Francisco, from the shelter I had so carefully crafted. It was all at once sudden and urgent, and the force of it pulled me to my feet. "I... I have to go." I started scanning for my keys.

It was only at this point that I noticed that Matt had been lost in his own world of shock and grief, but upon my standing he looked at me, frantic. "Alyssa, please, can we talk about this?"

But I had found my keys and was halfway to the door.

"I'm sorry, Matt."

"Where are you going?"

I turned back one last time, sorry for the mess I had made, the mess I was about to make. "I'm going home."

* * *

IT HAD BEEN YEARS SINCE I had felt the cool, humid air of Washington, and I rolled the windows down despite the rain, desperate to fill my lungs with it. With every breath I felt more and more alive, and with every landmark I passed another memory came roaring back into my consciousness to join the other revived ones that I had been trying to suppress for so long with futility.

I couldn't hide them. I saw that now. The truth of

that made me furious with myself for living a lie for so long. No matter how I tried to run away from my past, no matter how I tried to cling onto what I perceived to be a normal life, I couldn't escape from what I had lost. He was always there with me, in the inner dialogue that played through my head every time I felt my self-esteem slip, in every word of every essay that took me one step closer to my Masters degree. He was still there, my motivator and my barrier in everything I did. When Matt proposed to me, his words hitting against that impenetrable barrier, it made it all painfully clear. And I was furious.

I had told no one I was coming. I hadn't planned that far ahead. Pure feeling was what was propelling me, pushing me ever towards the last place my heart called home. As I drove down the shining streets, a rehearsal of what I would say, what I would do kept running through my mind. *How could you have done this to me? Don't you understand that I have never been able to love the same way since? Why did you never try to come find me? Did we mean nothing?*

I pulled up to that white house and clicked the engine off, not giving much time to gather my thoughts and put them in any rational order before I tumbled out of the driver's side door. It was only briefly that I was aware of the state of dress I was in, crumpled and stale from the plane ride, hair disheveled from pointless attempt to sleep against an unyielding cabin window. But then, what would he look like now? I could only imagine that these six years would have been kind to him, a slight dusting of gray at his temples to show the passage of time. Did he even still live here? What if he had moved on? Was I about to invade upon a family? One that he had built without me?

Only my indignation, my resolve to right a wrong and settle my past kept me walking up the pathway that led to the front door. There was no way for me to break through the barrier that was holding me back unless I confronted it with a hammer, so here I was, hammering at the door.

The silence that followed was close to unbearable, so I found myself continuing my pounding just so I didn't have to listen to my own racing thoughts. "Damn you, open the door!" I muttered to myself, almost to the point where my nerves would propel me away from the door, back into hiding...

But suddenly the door opened and Brian was there in front of me, surprise painting his features. "Alyssa!" He took a very deep breath, as if he were trying to keep from breaking down at the threshold. "I thought I would never see you again!"

I stood speechless, in shock of the fact that I was once again in the physical presence of him. I had lived for so long with his memory that having him within hand's reach made me feel dizzy. Studying his face, I could see that time had blessed him with his peppered temple, and when I looked into his eyes, I was saddened to see how tired his soul looked, and I couldn't help but feel my previous anger slipping away in favor of a stronger misery. I scanned over him, stopping at his left hand, looking for any indication...

"I'm not." He answered, knowing that I was checking for a ring. A brief flash of embarrassment seemed to sweep through him, and he looked away and studied the door jam. "There was never anyone else, Julietta."

I had to catch my breath, but as soon as I tried to exhale it was caught up in an involuntary sob. I feebly wiped at tears starting to run down my face, smearing my mascara and destroying my poorly constructed confidence. Realizing that I still had not yet said anything to him, I forced myself to open my mouth. "I..." The questions that had run through my head earlier now felt grossly inappropriate. "You ruined my life."

I felt weak, exposed. My attempt at living as if Brian had never existed had torn me apart at the seams, and now I was standing here, letting him know that my life was in shambles without him.

Somehow my meaning was clear to him, and he looked back down on me. After a moment a small smile that didn't quite reach his eyes appeared. It seemed that we had arrived at the irony of it all at the same time, and despite myself a coarse laugh escaped my lips. Brian responded with one of his own. "You ruined mine too." He countered.

This epiphany pressed down on both of us, demanding to be realized. Despite his good intentions and despite my efforts to move on, we were inexplicably placed back at the same doorway where we separated all those years ago. Still broken. Still incomplete. It was if fate called us out on our unconvincing lies and demanded a do-over.

I looked into his eyes, the dark, piercing eyes that had haunted my dreams, and found the forgiveness and comfort I had been desperately seeking elsewhere. Finally, I felt home. "Where do we go from here?" I asked, feeling overwhelmed from the enormity of the bridge we had at long last crossed.

Reaching out, he took my hand in his, and I savored his warmth as he shook my hand cordially. "Bueno, Me llamo Brian." (My name is Brian.)

"Me llamo Alyssa. Es un placer a conocerte." (My name's Alyssa. It's a pleasure to meet you.)

"Igualmente." (Likewise.)

Brian smiled at me, and I held on to his hand tightly as though he were an anchor.